the

danger

box

the da

SCHOLASTIC INC.
NEW YORK   TORONTO   LONDON   AUCKLAND
SYDNEY   MEXICO CITY   NEW DELHI   HONG KONG

BLUE BALLIETT

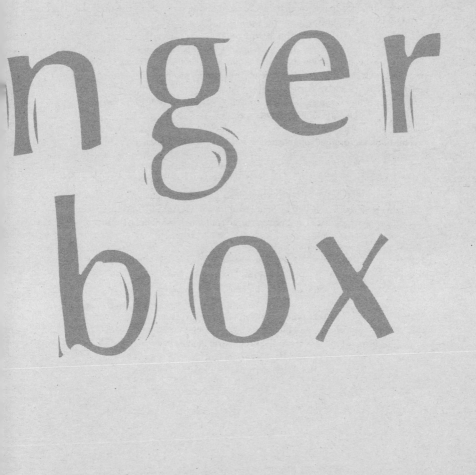

This book was originally published in hardcover by Scholastic Press in 2010.

ISBN 978-0-439-85210-4

12 11 10 9 8 7 6 5 4 3   15 16/0

Printed in the U.S.A.   40
First paperback printing, June 2012

The text type was set in Hoefler Text Roman
and Helvetica Neue Regular.
The display type was set in P22Prehistoric Pen, P22Victorian Swash,
and P22Victorian Gothic.
Book design by Marijka Kostiw

To

the

children

of

Three

Oaks

It is like confessing

a murder.

— Charles Darwin

His hand holding

the purple crayon

shook.

— Crockett Johnson

AUTHOR'S NOTE:
opening the box

ONE OF THE objects in *The Danger Box* is real. It was stolen from its owners a long time ago and is still missing. It is fragile, easily recognized around the world, too valuable to put a price on, and could fit in your pocket. In wondering where it is today and dreaming up this mystery, I also thought about how:

- Every book is a box of ideas.

- Every book that shares secrets is a Danger Box.

- One day someone really will find what is hidden in this book. It could be you.

CONTENTS

the game begins

Twelve words were painted in gold ink on the wall of an office in Dearborn, Michigan:

SURVIVAL	OF
	THE
	FITTEST
	IS
	A
	DEADLY
	GAME.
WHO CAN WIN	FOREVER?

Surrounding the message were exquisite photographs of mammals, birds, fish, reptiles, insects, and plants. Every color in the rainbow glistened from that wall, which felt alive; feathers ruffled, blossoms swayed, eyelashes blinked. The office belonged to a man known only as Mr. Zip — his real name had vanished decades earlier.

On the corner of his desk was a bowl made from a huge tortoiseshell. Inside, dozens of small glass cubes — each printed on six sides — twinkled in the light. Mr. Zip sometimes played with the cubes as if rolling dice.

He knew about survival, of course, but he might have forgotten how risky a secret could be. He was old, and felt he had earned the comfort of a short visit with an extraordinary treasure.

For a great deal of money, half of all he'd earned in a lifetime, Mr. Zip had bought the item from a private collection. He had asked no questions, and would give no answers.

Soon he'd be seen as a hero, for he had found and rescued a world-famous piece of human history, an item that had been missing for over twenty-five years. After a few magical days in its company, Mr. Zip's plan was to return the treasure to its original home. This was a challenge, an act of faith, and a final game: Mr. Zip would be remembered as a good and generous person, a man of heart as well as strategy. He hoped, in giving back this treasure to the world, to win forever. Didn't fame, after all, count as survival?

The plan was close to perfect.

He'd hired four players who had never met; each knew only his or her own role. A series of moves would deliver one small, sturdy box with a hinged top, a container about one-foot square. The outside was scratched and stained. The box had been sealed shut with heavy tape, then shrink-wrapped in clear plastic.

No one had counted on a fifth player: death. As the box traveled by boat across the Atlantic Ocean, a porthole threw a perfect circle of blinding light on its shiny top. Just at that moment, on a blue June day, Mr. Zip died. Final bubbles of air left his body as a burbling wake churned behind the boat, each moment carrying the box closer to its destination.

Mr. Zip's personal assistant was just pulling him from his swimming pool, where he'd suffered a fatal heart attack, when Player One handed the box to waiting arms in New York City. The player breathed deeply and set off to enjoy a day in Manhattan before flying back to London.

Soon Player Two was crossing Pennsylvania in a rented car, the box on the front seat beside him. Next, it rode with Player Three, humming along in a delivery van as far as Toledo, Ohio.

The final leg of the trip was in a new Ford truck, one with an empty gun rack, from Toledo into Michigan. Player Four had instructions to proceed directly to Flint, watching to be sure *he wasn't followed, and then double back toward a massive estate on the outskirts of Dearborn.*

Mr. Zip's assistant knew nothing about the delivery. He'd never heard of the plan, the players, or the box. He knew nothing about the complicated payment system, or the millions of dollars set to be released from a bank outside the United States.

Mr. Zip had told no one, not one living soul, about his scheme. He had counted on survival.

That, as it turned out, was a mistake; death changed all the rules.

Soon the game included Zoomy, Lorrol, a boy named Gas, a drunk, a stranger, and a small town in Michigan — that is, if it could still be called a game.

4

zoomy's box

I'M PULLING THE Danger Box out from the back of the toolshed. Now I'm crouching by the rakes and hoes. It's a windy June night, and the shadows from the kitchen light are bumping and chasing. I'm alone, at least I think I am. I open the box, a small cherry crate, and a tangy whiff of gunpowder drifts out.

Inside are pieces of blown-up firecrackers and a few old shotgun shells. I don't need to see them; I know the contents by touch. Each year I add stuff. Now I close my eyes and dig down into the mixture.

Yes! I feel the fabric and beneath it, a firm shape.

"Poor thing, I'm sorry you're buried out here," I whisper.

I tap my chin while I count to twelve, one number for each year of my life. *Dut, dut* goes the tapping. *Swish, whoosh* — now the sounds of summer in the big trees over the toolshed.

As I'm about to slide the box back in its hiding place, I hear footsteps. Uh-oh, not Grandpa Ash. Or Grandma

Al. I feel around, grab the nail on the edge of the toolshed door, and slowly pull the door closed. If I pull too fast it will squeak. Squeaks and secrets don't go together.

I hold my breath. *Thump-squish, thump-scree, thump-squish.* It's a man — I can tell by the weight of his steps.

It's dark in the shed, as speckly-dark as black pepper. *Thump, whump, thump!* My heart feels like a firecracker that's about to go off. I pretend my heart is in the Danger Box, and has already exploded.

i arrive

I HAVE ALWAYS lived in Three Oaks, Michigan. Or almost always: I was a few days old when I turned up on the kitchen steps of my grandparents' house one spring morning. Wrapped in an old sweatshirt, the arms tied together to keep me cozy, I was inside a cat carrying case. The door was shut. My Grandma Al says that this was smart.

A piece of paper with unfamiliar handwriting was taped to the top of the case. My grandma still has it. One word is spelled wrong, but someone worked hard to make the message as neat as a canning label:

Buckeye Chamberlain Is My Father
My Name Is Zoomy
Kep Me Please

Grandma Al was first in the kitchen that morning, and she heard a funny sound coming from outside. She opened the back door, and the rest is history. By the time my Grandpa Ash thumped downstairs to the kitchen, Gam — that's what I call her — was sitting at the kitchen table with me in her arms. She had tears running down her cheeks.

"Good Lord, whadda we have here?" my grandpa thundered. Gumps — that's the name I gave him — always shouts, because he can't hear well. He looked at the carrying case. "That a barn cat or a kid?"

"This is Zoomy," my grandma said. "He's ours."

secret times three

MY GRANDPA HAD some doubts, I guess, but he tried not to let on. I came with a full head of black hair and was the brown of an autumn acorn. In the shock of the moment, he couldn't figure that out. He'd never seen an unpink member of the family.

He scratched his head and just kept saying, "But his name is Zoomy," and then, "Well, I'll be. If turtles have wings!" Gumps only says that when he's one hundred percent amazed.

I should tell you who Buckeye is, and what Zoomy was, and then you'll understand how they knew I was me.

Buckeye is their son, and their only child. He'd been gone for eight months when I turned up. My grandparents had checked the mailbox and hoped for a phone call day after day, then week after week. They'd been real worried — Buckeye was only nineteen.

He was hard to tame, as Gumps put it, and drove the family truck so fast it got wrapped around more than one tree. He drank stuff he wasn't supposed to drink. He liked staying out late with girls. There were fistfights and word fights. He got in trouble both at school and with the police, partly because he always blamed someone else for what went wrong. He thought other people were trying to hurt him even if they were trying to help. He wanted to be good, as Gam said, but just didn't seem to know when enough was enough. Or when to trust. Or when to quit teasing.

"Teasing!" Gumps snorted. "How about breakin' the law?" Gam always bobbed her head around like her shirt collar didn't fit when he said things like that.

After leaving high school, Buckeye had moved over twenty miles down the road to live in the top of a peach grower's barn and work in his orchards. That was in the town of Berrien Springs.

Then my grandparents got a call. Buckeye had missed three days of work. His boss reported that one afternoon he had just plain walked off through the trees. He didn't come back.

Months went by. No calls, no letters. My grandpa called it the Waiting for Buckeye time, and said it hung like a wet morning on the house. That spring day when Gumps came downstairs to find no coffee but Gam sobbing happily in a chair — I guess that was the first wonderful dawn in a long time.

Zoomy was the name their son Buckeye had called his best friend, his *invisible* best friend, when he was a kid. He'd loved Zoomy to pieces. There was no mistaking that name.

That's where I came in. No one outside of our family knew the name Zoomy; Gam had taught her son to keep his friend a secret. That made me Real. A Gift. Maybe Buckeye told his girlfriend what he wanted to name their baby, or he'd shared stories about his childhood. Either way, it didn't matter to my grandparents. My name was all the proof they needed. I was clearly Buckeye's son.

I was the Secret from a Secret. The first had been the invisible Zoomy, of long ago, and now the second was the real Zoomy. Me.

Actually, my mother was a secret, too, so that made three: I was the Secret from a Secret from a Secret.

And all in a very small town.

our town

THREE OAKS HAS one main street. The train between Chicago and Detroit runs through the middle of the town but doesn't stop. It hasn't since 1959. On either side of Elm Street — that's the one with the stores — are parallel streets with blocks of wooden houses, two to the west and three to the east.

An old sign at the edge of town says:

WELCOME TO THREE OAKS
HAPPY TO HAVE YOU
SORRY TO SEE YOU GO

There's one official map and I know it by heart, north to south. Most of the streets are named after trees:

-Pine
-Chestnut
-Walnut
-Buckeye

-Butternut

-Hickory

-Cherry

-Poplar

-Beech

-Sycamore

-Maple

-Elm

-Linden

-Ash

-Locust

-Orange

-Spruce

-Palm

-Oak

-Cedar

-Paw paw

-Magnolia

After the streets come huge fields of either corn or soybeans, depending on the year. Roads and lawns end suddenly in open land. There aren't many fences in Three Oaks. Property lines are mostly marked by crops and trees.

In the summer, it's short greens and tall greens and sometimes a smudge of other colors. In winter, it's squinty white, and sometimes deep when it looks flat. In early spring and late fall, the town gets brown and black, like an old photograph. I always keep a purple pen in my pocket to remind me of how strong and clear the world can be. It bounces around with my Daily List Book.

Purple is one of my secrets. It helps me imagine I can see more clearly than I really can.

purple and no

NO AND *PURPLE* go together. Both have the same rounded feeling in my mind.

I try to start each daily list with the word *purple* somewhere in the first line (like, -Put Purple Pen in Pocket) and the word *no* in the last line (-No Wearing Socks to Bed). That makes the two ends of each day fit like they're supposed to, like spoons in the silverware drawer.

Each day is a circle that begins with a *purple* and ends with a *no*.

My grandma says *no* tells the outside world to watch out for your toes, and *purple* is the color of believing.

15

if i was a sheet

I'D BE A goner without my lists. I love the way a list makes a big hodgepodge of things simmer down and behave. Gam says lists have been around since the beginning of time.

Besides my Daily List Book, I keep separate notebooks with lists of all sorts of other things: private secrets (P on the cover), stuff I want to research (R), names I like (N), bugs I've found or been given (B). I also have G (garden) and S (our family store). I've been doing this for a long time. I store all the notebooks in shoe boxes under my bed.

I put down things other people don't have to think about. Like -Get Up, -Get Dressed, -Make Bed, and all that kind of stuff. When something gets done, I like to cross it off that instant, no matter where I am.

Before lists, I got stuck all the time. If I knew I was supposed to do something, sometimes I just couldn't do it. Instead I pressed on my eyebrows over and over, tapped my chin a million times, or squeezed my elbows.

When I was real young I screamed if my grandparents tried to stop me.

Then my grandma realized that I just needed something special, something that was mine to do, before the necessary thing like going to school. She tried to help me figure out a routine, like stretching my arms and legs every morning before I got out of bed, but that didn't work too well — was it my left leg then right, or the other way around? Soon I was pinching each toe before I could put on my socks and then waving my glasses in a circle around each ear before putting them on. And if the circles weren't perfect, I had to keep waving until they were.

Things were starting to get pretty busy.

And then Gam fixed it. "Lists!" she exclaimed one day. "I'd be lost without them. Hodilly-hum." That's her way of saying *Amen*, *Thank Goodness*, and *That's the Way It Is*. She went right out and got me my first list notebook, a small one from the Three Oaks Pharmacy.

My grandpa and grandma aren't like me. They're more like sheets drying outside on a breezy day — they change directions without any fuss. But me, if I was a sheet and the wind blew me, I'd never stop flapping.

My grandparents learned a long time ago that even

the smallest changes can make me jittery-splat, as we call it. That's when my stomach starts jumping around like crazy and the rest of me gets stuck, usually tapping. When I was little, they had to warn me before Gumps got a new pair of boots, or before Gam cut my sand- wiches in half instead of in triangles, or before they bought me a new pair of pants. They still try to warn me about everything new. At least, everything they can see coming.

I want to live with them forever.

news

AS PLAYER FOUR *left the men's room in a roadside bar in Flint, Michigan, he heard someone say the name of the estate. His destination. The last item on the checklist.*

"What in heck —?" he muttered, sinking down on a bar stool. He looked up at the only person talking in the room, the TV newscaster.

And there it was: the famous main entrance, the grand front gates decorated not with lions but with gilded 1964 Mustang cars. He couldn't believe what he was hearing.

The owner of this famous home, Mr. Zip, had died. Heart condition. The announcer was just saying with a smile that he had been one of the wealthiest automobile manufacturers in the United States, a man without surviving family. A famous loner. Who would inherit his millions?

The man listening slapped the bar with one hand.

what i see

I LOOK DIFFERENT to other people from the way I see myself in a mirror, and they look different to me. We don't see the same. I'm not one hundred percent blind, but my eyes have what's called Pathological Myopia, and I'm *legally* blind. My grandparents call it a good thing that we can say it, because it gets me lots of help for free.

Stick your finger straight out from the tip of your nose: That's how far I can focus clearly. To see farther, I have to put on my glasses, which are heavy. The lenses are about as thick as a homemade oatmeal cookie, and the frames are brown. With glasses, you can see my whole eye and I guess it looks far away, like it's maybe in the next room. That's called an Optical Illusion. From my side, the glasses let me see exactly an arm's length in front of my face, but the stuff on the edges looks bendy even if it's straight. When I'm older, my grandma says I can get glasses that work like a telescope, and maybe even contact lenses. She says that by then they'll have more inventions for people like me.

I mostly take off my glasses to read and see anything else up close. They have a stretchy purple cord so they can hang around my neck and not get lost. When I'm looking at something like words, I move my head back and forth, back and forth. My face is often so close to things that I notice smells other people don't, like the delicious scent in the binding of a new book. Gam says I'm the family hound. That's because of my determination — once I start on something I never want to stop — and my expert nose.

I'm shorter than other kids my age, and I have thick hair that grows north, south, east, and west, even after a buzz cut. Gumps, who doesn't have much hair, says I'm lucky to have it.

I have veins that don't look blue through the skin on my hands, and I don't get sunburned like my grandparents do. We all think I have more practical skin than the other Chamberlains. When we look at pictures of Buckeye, the three of us think I have his exact same chin and toes. And the curly smile he had when he was a little boy. At home there's a framed picture of him in a cowboy outfit on Elm Street, holding a huge lollipop. He looks like a kid who might be my friend but of course that's impossible. If we were on a big family list, he'd be on one line and I'd be on another much later on, because we're divided by a ton of crossed-off years in between.

When I learned how to walk, before they knew I had Pathological Myopia, I fell a lot and crashed off stairs and curbs. I broke an arm and a bunch of fingers. Then I got my first glasses and that helped lots. But I can't ride a bike down the street or play ball, at least with anything smaller than a beach ball. Besides, when you have my kind of eyes you're not supposed to do rough sports or smack your head — a huge jolt could make your sight even worse.

Gumps set up an awesome bike that stays out on the screen porch at the back of the house. It's stuck on a heavy base so it doesn't go anywhere, but it has gears, brakes, and an adjustable seat. It even has a bell. I can use it all year, even in the coldest weather, and when I ride on windy days it feels like I'm speeding along. I think it's better than a regular bike, because you can't slip on leaves or ice and you don't have to worry about cars.

One day I was reading a book about how bodies are put together, and how each human has a unique combination of traits. I like that word, *traits*. Suddenly I got an amazing idea, and here it is: I don't know how anyone else sees the world, and no one else knows exactly how I see the world! We each see in our own, unique way. There isn't a Right or a Wrong, and that's how it's meant to be. Maybe this means that it's fair getting any kind of vision you happen to get. If you can see More, it isn't always Better. Just different.

Who knows, I might see more detail up close than other people do. Maybe they miss a lot because they're so busy looking far away. I know that a piece of bread has tiny bowls in it and a hand has lines like the rivers on a map. Paper in a book isn't smooth — it has marks that remind me of footprints on gravel. And if you lie on your stomach in the grass, you'll be shocked at everything going on; it's truly a jungle.

I'll bet most people don't know how interesting everyday stuff is if you look closely. The only reason I do is my different kind of seeing.

23

corners and rounds

GAM SAYS SHE can't think without sorting. She calls me her Number One tidier and helper.

I reorganized the kitchen so that most things with corners (cereal boxes, crackers, breadboard, tea bags) are in one area, and all the round things (juice glasses, salt and pepper shakers, spice bottles, pots and frying pans) are in another. Things with corners are harder to figure out than things that are round.

My grandma leaves a fresh stack of my notebooks on the kitchen counter near the place mats and a handful of identical purple pens in a jar near the spices. That way I'm ready for anything.

"Lists make sense out of a mess," Gam likes to say. She sits at the kitchen table and writes her words on a long pad with a magnet. Then she sticks it to the refrigerator. Sometimes she tears off a page and puts it in her pocket when she leaves the house.

Her lists are shorter than mine. They're about things

she might not remember, and mine are about things I can't forget. Here's one of hers:

-Ivory Soap
-Seasoned Salt
-Rice
-Lard

Here's one of mine, the morning part:

-Bring Purple Pen Downstairs
-Have Cornflakes & Raspberries in Yellow Bowl
-Check for Flower Blossoms in Front
-Water Garden in Back
-Help Shake Out & Hang Laundry

I just learned that "&" sign and love to use it. Gam calls it Efficient. She and I are both more relaxed when we get to cross off a list item by item. Sometimes I use a line; sometimes a check; sometimes an *X*.

My grandma says keeping a list is like stepping on one stone and then another to get across a stream. Even if the stones are different sizes or slippery, it's better than jumping into the stream and not knowing if it's over your head. Sometimes lists make me think about Harold, from *Harold and the Purple Crayon*, a picture book that I still love.

My copy says *Buckeye Chamberlain* inside, written in messy, little-kid letters. I added *Zoomy Chamberlain* right underneath.

In this book, Harold draws himself into an adventure and then draws himself out of it. He concentrates hard while he's drawing, and he makes his world do what he wants it to do.

I wonder if he also kept lists.

think!

PLAYER FOUR WAS thinking. Thinking hard.

This job had been an easy one, with the promise of excellent pay. He had no idea what was in the box, but knew it must be priceless; the instructions had been unusually hush-hush. Supposedly, no one but Mr. Zip knew all of the players and their moves. But now . . .

Having ordered a burger and fries with orange soda, the player picked at his meal and tried to ignore the only other customer in the bar, a young man who had clearly had too much to drink and was babbling about having lost his job in one of the automotive plants.

Player Four took a sip of his drink. If he kept the box, would anyone miss it? Would someone come after him? Why would Mr. Zip have gone to all the trouble if this weren't the treasure of a lifetime?

If he went ahead and delivered it, who knew what would happen? He might be arrested. Or he could be handing it over for no pay. But if he disappeared . . .

Tempting — it was truly tempting.

It was also a gamble.

The drunk left first, after muttering something about survival. The player asked for his bill. He'd made a decision.

Stepping outside minutes later, he took a deep breath of evening air. The sky was a delicious, bottomless blue — the last blue before dark. The color of a sapphire. Tonight he was a poet; he could afford to be. He might be on his way to becoming a wealthy man.

Walking happily toward the parking lot behind the building, he looked for the first star. He hadn't thought of this rhyme since he was a kid:

STAR LIGHT, STAR BRIGHT,
FIRST STAR I SEE TONIGHT.
I WISH I MAY, I WISH I MIGHT
HAVE THIS WISH I WISH TONIGHT.

He made a silent wish and chuckled to himself, shaking his head. Then, turning the corner of the building, he stopped dead. How could this be?

He dashed back into the bar.

"My truck!" he shouted at the bartender. "It's gone!"

deeps

COLORS ARE IMPORTANT, maybe because I can see them even without the shapes. Distances and spaces are complicated. As Gam explains it, everyone learns how to judge the distances between things, but most people can easily tell how deep the water is in a bathtub just by looking at it. I had to learn by putting my arm down into it. That's when I started using the word *Deep*.

When I was little, my grandparents said I thought everything was made up of Deeps — there was a Deep of sky, and a huge outside Deep of green or brown or white, depending on the seasons. I sometimes still think trees are like the stitches in one of my grandma's old quilts, and that they hold the Deeps together. They grab the sky but also reach into the earth and hold on to that, too.

Because of who I am and how I see, my life has many kinds of secrets, things other kids just might not know. I don't have many out-of-family friends, not close ones, but I don't mind. My buddies are my grandparents and some of my special things — my notebooks and the collection in the Danger Box.

But just this summer, the friend list has changed.

There's Gas.

And Lorrol.

enter gas and lorrol

GAS IS HIS secret name.

He's no longer alive. Gas was his nickname when he was young.

He's the kind of friend kids dream about: never boring or mean, and not so perfect he gets you discouraged. The kind of guy who makes you believe you might get things done in the world. Like your ideas might matter, even if you're not sure what those ideas are. Like you might even be famous one day, too.

He's good company even though we can't exactly talk. He had jittery-splat moments his whole life, and he understood how a secret could be both good and bad.

Lorrol is different. She's still one hundred percent alive. She's like a rare beetle, the kind with iridescent colors and pincers. Fascinating, powerful, and possibly explosive: You have to watch out. She's not exactly predictable, but she makes things happen.

It was Lorrol's idea to start the *Gas Gazette*.

The Gas Gazette: Issue One

A FREE NEWSPAPER ABOUT A MYSTERIOUS SOUL

~I was born before Three Oaks.

~My mother died when I was eight years old.

~I wasn't very good at school. Here's what I wrote about it later: "School as a means of education to me was simply a blank."

~Sometimes I lied. Once I stole valuable peaches and plums from my father's orchard and left them in a pile, then "discovered" it. No one believed me.

~When I was very little I remember being shut in a room for bad behavior and breaking a window. On purpose.

~I loved hunting when I was young. My father once said to me, "You care for nothing but shooting, dogs, and rat catching, and you will be a disgrace to yourself and all your family."

Who am I?

NEXT ISSUE TO COME.

FREE!

good-bye troll

UNTIL GAS AND Lorrol, most of my experiences with other kids were not fun at all.

Once Gam invited a boy down the street to come play. I thought we could make a baking soda volcano, which I'm really good at doing. He just wanted to jump on my bed and throw things. Then he tried on my glasses and asked if he looked like a weirdo, too. Next he made up a game: I was the mad scientist with shrunken eyes who wanted to catch him and turn him into a troll. He called me Slowpokey and Inchwormy instead of Zoomy.

Running to the other side of my room, he kept saying, "Which finger am I sticking up?" I couldn't see his hand. When I explained that, he started a game of hide-and-seek with something larger, a dictionary. He re-hid it over and over before I got close, saying "duh" like it was so obvious. I knew he was smiling — if someone talks and smiles at the same time, I can hear it. When his mom picked him up, I crossed the Troll off my list right away. Before they were even out the door. Gam told me that looked rude, and I was glad.

My grandma has always said that when I'm older, I'll be able to go to a special school just for teens who are legally blind, and it'll be much easier to make close friends. She once told me that most people think everyone sees the world just as they do, and that's why some kids are impatient or unkind. They can't understand what *I* see any better than a bird flying overhead can understand what *they* see. Then she said hodilly-hum, and I hugged her extra hard.

the search box

AT SCHOOL I stay in the Special Room. It has paper stars all over the door, and a name inside each star.

I'm not in the regular classroom because I wouldn't be able to see the blackboard, most of the other kids, or the teacher. This way, I don't have to worry about what I'm missing. Kids in our school say hi to me in the hall and I always say hi back, but they move very quickly. Sometimes I'm not sure who's speaking.

I'm glad I have a separate place to go at school. And I feel like one of the lucky ones; some of the kids in the Special Room have a much harder time.

Once I brought a cicada in a jar and showed it to a girl with long, skinny braids. I thought she'd like that because she always carries a stuffed ladybug. I bumped her elbow by mistake when we were looking, and she bit my ear. Hard. The jar fell on the floor and broke and I never saw the cicada again.

The kids in our room don't mean to have those bad

things happen, it's more like they can't help it. The world gets them so fizzed up, they can't think straight.

Most of them don't like to talk or read much, and they're happiest if they can do things on their own. I've learned to mind my own business and stay at my round table in the corner.

That's where I do regular school stuff with my very own teacher, Mrs. Fufty. She's nice and looks like a twice-baked potato, the kind that puffs out of its jacket. Sometimes she brings yellow stickers with a smiley face and puts them on the back of my hand. She gives me assignments to finish when she's not there. I also get lots of computer time, which is the absolute best thing about being at school.

I like computers because:

-They don't jump around.
-They never get tired of doing what you want them to do.
-They know more details than anyone alive.

I'm nuts about the Search Box. All I do is type in a subject or a name, and lots of cool stuff pops up. I click on what I want to read, and that leads me to something else. Sometimes I imagine a huge tree inside the Search Box — I climb in and inch along one branch, then crawl to another, and on and on. Not that I've ever seen the details up in a really big tree, but I've seen plenty of pictures and stood next to the trunks. I know those branches are up there.

When I read or hear a name I like, I put it in the list book marked N. Then I look it up and see what I can find about the person. Some of my favorites are Al Capone, Marie Curie, Django Reinhardt, and Black Elk. It's sort of like a treasure hunt.

If Mrs. Fufty is watching, I use books before the computer. She loves to say, "The *In*ternet is *Not* Always *Ac*curate," and the way she says it makes it sound like a weird song.

If she's not around, I jump right in. The Search Box allows anyone to become a spy.

The Gas Gazette: Issue Two

A FREE NEWSPAPER ABOUT A MYSTERIOUS SOUL

~I made up this code and wrote it down in a note-book when I was somewhere between ten and twelve.

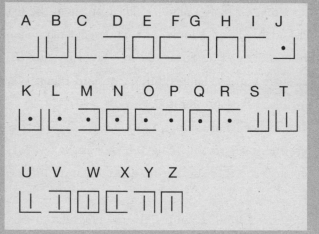

Who am I?

Can you write your name in my code?

NEXT ISSUE TO COME.

FREE!

broken things

WE DON'T HAVE a TV at home. It broke when I was little, and my grandma was glad. When it worked, I had to sit a couple of feet away to see it. She says being that close to electronics can scramble your brains, and she doesn't want mine to turn into an omelet.

Once one of the other kids in the Special Room, a guy who's much bigger than me, grabbed my Daily List Book and dropped it down his pants. Then he ran into the bathroom and flushed the toilet about ten times. I think he just wanted me to pay attention to him and not my notebook, but it didn't work. My notebook broke the toilet. Then my stomach got so jittery I couldn't do anything but stand in one place and tap my chin like mad until Gam arrived. She brought me a new notebook and I sat down again and wrote -Start New List. That was my only Really Rough Day at school.

I like being home because I can relax and I know where everything is and when stuff will happen. And I never have to worry about being understood.

At least, I never did until my discovery. A secret can be a Deep that is really hard to see. That's what I was doing in the toolshed with the Danger Box. Trying to do the right thing.

Sometimes I think it would be good to be an already-exploded firecracker: It would be a relief. Even with Gas and Lorrol around.

BANG! No decisions. No worries about things getting broken.

a teapot and a pail

I WOULD HAVE exploded long ago without:

-Gam and Gumps.

My grandma's real name is Alice Turner Chamberlain. Because I see people up close and in sections, not all at one time, I picture them as being like something smaller. Sometimes I also picture a person as a color.

Gam is shaped just like a teapot, only she's squishy. Squishy in a sofa pillow way. And she's smooth like baby powder. She smells like lavender. I help her plant lavender along the side of the house every summer, once the soil is warm. Lavender flowers are secretive and very purple, so they are my favorite flower. Unless you're a bee or a boy with Pathological Myopia, you might miss these flowers completely. You have to be up close to see them.

My grandma's inside color feels like green, the gentle kind you see on a maple seedling. She knows how to say and do things that land in the right spot, like they belong. Even the way she screws the top on or off a jam jar seems perfect: the twist, twist, and firm letting go. This looks magical to me — I'm always bumping and tripping, and need to touch stuff before I decide what to do with it. I guess Gam understands most puzzles instantly. She makes the world seem like a safe and happy place, a place where many things are possible and there's always a hug waiting. A hug plus a hodilly-hum. And some homemade blueberry jam, the kind with whole berries in it.

My grandpa's real name is Ash Baker Chamberlain. He and Gam were both born in Three Oaks, and their families go back for generations. Our family business, Chamberlain Antiques and Whatnots, started off as my grandfather's father's business. It's been on Elm Street, next to the Gun Shop, for much longer than anyone living can remember. Gam took a job dusting in the store when she was in high school, and things went on from there.

Gumps is loud, big, and unsquishy. He has a wrinkly forehead and neck. I think his perfect color might be a strong blue, like the flowers that grow wild at the edge of the cornfields in summer. He makes me think of a big scrubbing pail, maybe because he's strong and smells like metal, and once in a while he clanks. There's steel inside his left arm, and he wears an aluminum foot on his right leg. He was blown up in the Vietnam War, which was a long time ago. I think that's why he doesn't like firecrackers. The war is also where he lost a lot of his hearing.

Sometimes he tries to nip Gam on the nose, and she shoos him away like a bad fly. He always waits until he sees her busy with both hands in the dishes or kneading the bread, something like that.

"Watch out!" I yell if I see him creeping close, but it's usually too late.

He tries to sneak up on me and wrestle with my ears. That's because my hearing is so good, and he says he wants some of it. Sometimes we do thumb wars on the kitchen table until Gam makes us stop because the table is bouncing.

"You boys!" she'll say. "You're hopeless creatures!"

Then Gumps always says, "I aim to take advantage," which for some reason sounds very funny and we all laugh.

My grandparents have lived in our house on Oak Street since they were married. My grandma was born in the house. It's the only place she's ever lived.

When Buckeye turned up at the kitchen door one evening a few weeks ago, it felt like the world tipped and the floor lost its flatness.

It seemed like the sugar bowl spilled and no one even noticed.

surprise

GAM GASPED AND covered her mouth with the dish towel. I was standing at the sink, passing her the wet plates.

Gumps had just tied the garbage bag and was getting ready to take it out. He boomed, "Good Lord above! Well, if turtles have wings!"

My stomach dropped into its panic mode — it felt like a bug trapped in a jar. I suddenly knew who this was, and I -didn't, -didn't, -didn't want to go jittery-splat in front of him. I held my breath and began tapping my chin.

I felt Gam's hand on my shoulder, and the next thing I knew, the man was giving her a hug. He reached across me, turned on the cold water, and bent over to drink right out of the tap. He gulped and swallowed for what seemed like forever. I could see the stubble on his neck sliding up and down, up and down. He smelled like an old adhesive bandage, one that hadn't dried after a soak in the tub.

I was still tapping.

Next thing I knew, I heard him saying, "Who's this? Neighbor's kid?" Then he made a nasty, choked-up sound and spat into the sink. He had messy hair that looked like he'd been sleeping inside a bramble patch. It was the same color as dead grass.

Right then Gumps boomed, "Let's go out to the garden, son! Lots to catch up on." And the back door slammed.

Gam gently pushed me down in a kitchen chair. "You can get out your list book now" was all she said.

no room

I DID, AND wrote ~Buckeye Walks In, squashing it in tiny letters between ~Eat Dinner and ~Take Shower. Then I crossed it off. My hand was so sweaty it was hard to hold the pen.

Gam ran hot water in the sink where Buckeye had spat. "Well, good heavens," she said. "This is certainly a surprise!"

Usually she then says stuff like, "Surprises are a necessary part of life, just like a winter storm," or "Surprises are like a bit of eggshell in a cake — you gotta love them, because they go with what makes the cake so good." She was full of those kinds of sayings, things that made life smoother . . . but not at this moment.

Next we heard shouting coming through the open window.

"How the HECK should I know?" Buckeye's voice sounded crusty. Some nasty words were followed by, "No WAY! You're an old fool if you think —"

Gam reached over quickly to turn on the radio just

as Gumps roared, "Dang-blast it all! What on EARTH is wrong with you?"

Buckeye shouted, "I DON'T KNOW! That make you happy?"

Gam said in a shaky voice, "Can't imagine what this fuss is all about," and tried to smile at me. She gripped the back of a kitchen chair with both hands, and I could see the tips of her fingers go from pink to white.

Suddenly the shouting was over and the voices stopped. I watched my grandma set plates for dessert and pull out a half of a strawberry-rhubarb pie. Then she plunked down the Cool Whip and stuck a trembly spoon in it. I got up and pecked out the kitchen window, but couldn't see far enough to tell what was going on. Shapes moved in front of something bright red.

Gam looked out, too, and said, "Buckeye unloaded a box from his pickup. Your grandpa stuck it in the garage."

Suddenly I realized what that might mean, and my stomach started doing its bug-in-a-tight-spot routine. Neither of us said anything like, "I hope he can stay for a while," or "Isn't it great to have him home!" It seemed like the kitchen was so full of worries there wasn't room for words.

eyebrow

THE TWO MEN came back inside. Gumps said, "Buckeye brought us some things for the store."

"That's nice. Thank you, son," Gam said quietly.

The four of us sat down at the kitchen table, and I sneaked a good look at Buckeye's face.

It made me think of a rotten zucchini, or a cucumber left out in the fields after the first frost. Buckeye had squishy-looking skin and black circles under his eyes. A dark, bumpy scar ran along one cheek. It jumped over his eye and went right up through his eyebrow, chopping it in half. I remembered when Gumps took me fishing once and cut a worm in half for bait. Both ends still wiggled. I wondered if Buckeye's eyebrow worked the same way.

He didn't look anything like the boy in the picture, the boy with the lollipop.

I wasn't hungry. Buckeye bent over his plate and ate noisily, pausing every once in a while to shake his head. Then his chair creaked. He turned my way. I looked

48

down at my notebook, which was always next to me on the table at mealtimes.

Suddenly a big hand flew across my plate and grabbed the notebook. I froze.

Buckeye read aloud, "'Get up, Go to School'? 'Buckeye Walks In'?" He snorted. "What is this kid, a nut?"

I began tapping my chin at top speed, and then everything happened at once.

Gumps stood up so fast his chair tipped over. "Hey! That's ENOUGH!" Each word was louder than the one before.

Gam said in a voice that sounded like scissors snipping paper, "Give. Back. That. Notebook. *Now*."

Buckeye's arm flew out in a quick arc, and I heard the soft *plonk* of something landing in the garbage can by the back door. "Slam dunk!" Buckeye said. "Trash from trash!"

Suddenly he was up and out of the kitchen, the screen door banging noisily behind him. We heard his truck revving, and then a squeal of tires and a *thumpa-bump* as he drove over the railroad tie that separated Gam's flowers from the driveway.

I was still tapping my chin when Gumps fished my notebook out of the garbage and wiped it off with a sponge. He handed it to me and I wrote -Buckeye Leaves and put a line through that, too. My purple pen was shaking. Gam was still in her chair at the table. She whispered, "Lord God above. You know we love you, Zoomy."

I nodded.

horseshoe

THAT NIGHT, LONG after I'd heard Gumps lock both the front door and the back, something he never does, I still couldn't sleep.

A wind came up, and the oak trees outside seemed to be moaning. I couldn't help wondering if Buckeye was sad or mad or both because he wasn't sleeping in his old room. Had my grandpa told him it was now my room? I hoped not. I wondered if Buckeye was sleeping in the truck. Then I also wondered how he'd gotten that big scar on his face. I felt a little sorry for him.

A frightening thought popped into my head: What if Buckeye had been telling Gumps that I wasn't his kid? But if I wasn't his kid, what about the sign on the cat carrier? And who knew Buckeye well enough to know about his secret friend, Zoomy?

Would I suddenly not be a real part of the family if I weren't Buckeye's son?

The more I pushed the idea away, the more it came

back, like snapping a rubber band over and over. I began tapping my chin.

What - tap! *If* - tap! *What* - tap! *If* - tap! *What* - tap! *If* - tap!

Sometime during the night, I passed out.

At dawn, a hard rain pounded the roof. It left a puddle the shape of a horseshoe where Buckeye's tires had sunk into Gam's garden. A horseshoe should be lucky.

The Gas Gazette: Issue Three

A FREE NEWSPAPER ABOUT A MYSTERIOUS SOUL

~I've always been a dreamer. Once I was walking along a high wall and thinking so hard about something that I fell off. I remember being amazed at all the thoughts I had during that second or two that I was falling.

~I started collecting things when I was little. At first it was stamps, coins, rocks, plant leaves, shells, and sea creatures.

~Later, I became fascinated by beetles. When I started a project, I never wanted to stop, even if other people did. I think my thoughts are the kind that get stuck and stay there for a while. Whatever it is I'm doing, I think it's the most important thing in the world. Sometimes that's a good thing.

~This is what I wrote about one collecting adventure: "One day, on tearing off some old bark, I saw two rare beetles and seized one in each hand; then I saw a third and new kind, which I could not bear to lose. . . . I popped the one which I held in my right hand into my mouth. Alas! It ejected some intensely acrid fluid, which burnt my tongue so that I was forced to spit the beetle out, which was lost, as was the third one."

~You could say I don't give up easily.

Who am I?

NEXT ISSUE TO COME.

FREE!

stinging

"WHAT HAPPENED TO your chin, Zoomy?" Grandma Al's voice was so kind that tears began prickling behind my glasses. Pretty soon a couple escaped. I stirred my cereal around in the bowl as if everything was fine. A tear ran past my chin and stung where the skin was sore from tapping.

"What if I'm not really a Chamberlain?" I whispered. I wanted to say more, but was too jittery-splat and miserable to get any extra words out.

Next thing I knew, Gam was hugging me. She called to Gumps. He thumped into the kitchen and squeezed my shoulder. The three of us had a talk.

They told me some things they hadn't seen any reason to share when I was younger. They told me that after Buckeye disappeared so long ago, the peach farmer he'd worked for said he soon realized that one of the girls at the farm, a young migrant worker from Mexico or Texas, was pregnant. Everyone said she was having Buckeye's kid. She left the farm before the baby was born. Her boss didn't know where she went, and she didn't come back the next season.

I guess the farmer always paid his workers in cash and never asked if they were living legally in the United States. That way he had help, they had work, and no one got in trouble. He only knew that her name was Abelina.

Abelina. I felt like the word had *!!* after it. It made my brain sting.

When Gumps asked Buckeye yesterday if he knew I was his kid, he thought that was crazy. He did remember a girl with that name, but he didn't remember much else.

"Yep," my grandpa said, and rubbed his face in a tired way with the palm of his hand. "I'm afraid Buckeye is a heavy drinker, and it's tough to help people like that accept responsibility for whatever they've been doing, because they can't remember most of it."

Accept responsibility sounded bad. . . . Did that mean Gumps wanted Buckeye to suddenly turn into my dad? And if he turned into my dad, could he take me away? That couldn't be what my grandpa wanted!

The tear faucet started again, and when Gam grabbed my hand to stop the tapping, I whispered, "No No No

NO!" over and over. They asked me a bunch of questions, but nothing was right.

No, I wasn't upset because Buckeye didn't believe he had a son.

No, I wasn't upset because he wasn't nice to me.

No, I wasn't upset because I might never meet my mom.

No, no, NO!

Finally I blurted it out: "I don't want Buckeye! I don't *want* him to accept!"

"Oh, Zoomy!" Gumps boomed. "I just meant I wanted him to grow up, that's all."

Gam put her face down close to mine. "Don't you wor-ry," she said, cutting the syllables into tidy chunks. "You are our very own Secret from a Secret, our very own blessing, and that's just the way we like it. Gumps and I would never allow anyone to take you. Never. Do you hear me, Zoomy?"

I nodded. But I also noticed she didn't say *grandchild*. For the first time ever, being a Secret didn't feel perfect.

worry crumbs

ALL OF THIS talk had left a sprinkling of worries in my mind, even though I believed my grandparents.

Gam calls them worry crumbs, those leftover bits of an uncomfortable idea. She fixes worry crumbs with sayings, and she has one to fit almost any size mess or confusion. Here are two of her favorites:

-Life is a blessing, and you get what you can handle. (That's to help you plow ahead and not whine.)

-The Rule is simple: Always treat other people the way you'd like to be treated. (That means pretend you're the other person and see how it feels.)

But how did Buckeye fit in? Hadn't he been taught all the same stuff when he was a kid? How could he have turned out so mean? I thought again about some of the things I'd just learned about Buckeye.

My grandparents said he had started out a happy kid and then turned stormy, the kind of storm that blows up out of nowhere. "Until he was ten or eleven, he was fine,"

Gam said. "Got along with everyone, even liked school. Then things started to fall apart for him. One moment he'd be riding his bike happily, and the next, everything was wrong, like someone had done something to him — kinda like the whole world was one huge mosquito bite and he couldn't stop being upset about it." She sighed, shaking her head.

One by one, Buckeye lost his friends. He scared everyone away. My grandparents took him to the family doctor, who said that some kids just have a hard time growing up. And then Zoomy appeared; not me, the first one. Well, he didn't appear, he somehow popped out of Buckeye's mind, and one morning came downstairs with him for pancakes.

No one but Buckeye could see or hear Zoomy, but he turned into such an important part of the family that my grandma always set a place for him at the kitchen table. Although Zoomy stayed a Chamberlain secret, I guess he seemed real enough at home. Gam and Gumps said Buckeye would eat his supper, then run around the table and eat Zoomy's supper. Buckeye and Zoomy helped each other with chores, went out to play, even told each other jokes. Zoomy was always there for Buckeye, and

Buckeye was at his best with Zoomy. This went on until Buckeye became a teenager and stopped talking, "at least at home," as Gumps growled. Zoomy kinda slipped out of sight — that is, if someone invisible can disappear.

Inside, I kept puzzling. Why had Buckeye stayed away for so long? Why was he always angry? And what would happen when he showed up again?

At least he wasn't happy to see me.

That was a very good thing. I couldn't imagine life without my grandparents. Not for half a minute, not for half a second. Not at all. I didn't *want* a father or a mother like other kids.

I spent the morning helping Gam hang laundry and stacking kindling in the backyard as fast as Gumps could split it.

Then I had an idea.

After lunch I asked, "Is it okay if I go to the library today?" I tried to sound casual.

I could feel Gam looking at me. "Hmmm" was all she said.

Then Gumps said, "I'm walking over that way anyway, so I'll go with you." It was Sunday and the store wasn't open.

"Thanks, Gumps," I said.

"You'll keep the house locked," I heard him saying to Gam. I couldn't see her face, but there was a moment of total quiet in the kitchen.

We all three understood: Buckeye felt dangerous.

The Gas Gazette: Issue Four

A FREE NEWSPAPER ABOUT A MYSTERIOUS SOUL

~At fifteen I was allowed to shoot a gun. Killing birds became a passion. I thought about shooting night and day.

~I left my hunting boots by the side of my bed so that I could wake up and slip them on without wasting a second.

~For years, I kept exact lists of each kind of bird I'd shot. I made up a system for when I was out in the field — I tied certain knots on a long string attached to a buttonhole in my jacket. As soon as I got home, I wrote down everything, translating the knots onto a chart.

~Once a group of friends played a trick on me. Every time they saw me aiming for a bird, they all shot their guns, too, until I didn't know what to count and what not to count. Then I realized they were just trying to mess up my counting and sorting system. Not everyone understands the beauty of lists.

~When I got older, I didn't like killing any living animal unless I had to do it.

~I started out wild. I turned tame. My wildness turned into words.

~I started out asking questions and kept asking them. Tons of them.

~Sometimes I answered them myself. Sometimes I couldn't.

~Questions are more fun than shooting.

Who am I?

NEXT ISSUE TO COME.

FREE!

featherbone

I'M AT HOME in the library even though it's not cozy.
Maybe that's because it's part of the history of Three
Oaks, and Three Oaks is part of me.

One of my great-something grandfathers, Henry
Chamberlain, started a sawmill in the wilderness not far
from here. It was near three huge oak trees that grew so
close they looked like a single tree. That was in the 1850s,
and most houses in the United States were built from
wood. Hardwood like oak and maple was the best, and
Michigan had plenty of that.

Soon Three Oaks was a small town with a main street,
the one that's still Elm. There was a general store, a couple of churches, and a schoolhouse. When you compare
the old photographs to now, it doesn't look too different — except for horses and wagons everywhere, muddy
roads, and grown-ups wearing suits and long dresses. The
train tracks were right where they are now and the buildings haven't changed a whole lot.

It was a small lumber town until a guy named E. K.

Warren invented something that made this place rich and famous. At least for a while. That something was called:

-Featherbone.

It was a bendy material made from turkey quills, and replaced whalebone corsets for women. (A corset is underwear that can squeeze a woman's waist until it gets tiny.) I guess featherbone was revolutionary. It was more comfortable to wear and much cheaper to make. Plus, it's way easier to catch a turkey than a whale.

Featherbone was also used in horsewhips. Women being squished and horses being hit: Not too nice-sounding a business, but I guess that's what people wanted.

After making some huge, brick factory sheds — a couple of them are still standing — Mr. Warren designed the fancy office building that's now our library. Gumps says old E. K. was trying to impress his customers. That's why there's marble on the floors and walls, a whoop-de-doo staircase right inside the front doors, places for chandeliers, and endless rooms with brass doorknobs. It was all that featherbone money.

When women stopped wearing corsets and cars were invented, the company shrank down. Featherbone was still used for making stiff collars and hems until the 1950s, when the business closed. The office building turned into a big museum celebrating Three Oaks, and at one time it had 80,000 artifacts from the pioneer and factory days, things like butter churns and quilting frames and bicycles with giant wheels. The place was named in honor of Henry Chamberlain.

I once saw a photograph of him. We both have a small nose and he wore glasses, too. If old Henry hadn't gotten excited about chopping down trees right on this spot, E. K. Warren might not have settled here, looked at a turkey feather, and thought up featherbone. And without that, Chamberlain Antiques and Whatnots might not have had treasures to sell. None of us would be here.

Our town is a mixture of luck and chance — with a few inherited traits and tools.

tools

OUR LIBRARY IS like a skinny person in a giant pair of pants; all the books fit on the first floor, and there is still plenty of room to spare. No one ever goes to the basement or third and fourth floors, and I've heard there's a ghost but I'd rather not think about that.

Until recently, a few computers were kept on the second floor. That's also where we have what's left of the old museum: mostly bread bowls and portraits of people who look like they might have a toothache. Gam says they probably did.

There's not much electricity upstairs, but one day my grandma and I were allowed to go inside the exhibit areas with a flashlight and a magnifying glass. I was crazy about the homemade tools, the ones used by the blacksmiths, woodworkers, coopers, and cobblers. Here is a list of favorites:

-Chisel
-Block Plane

-Jack Plane

-Surface Plane

-Maul

-Adze

-Shave

-Scraper

-Level

Most look sharp, heavy, and kind of scary. Like they belong in someone's Danger Box.

That Sunday, when Gumps and I went to the library, he stayed downstairs to read newspapers in a big chair and take a bird nap. He calls it that because he can do it sitting up with his beak closed. I climbed the big stairs to the computers, just down the hall from the tools. If the people who built houses, stores, and all kinds of wagons in Three Oaks could see this small tool in a lightweight box, they would flip. Tools weren't so easy to handle in those days.

Each one of the four computers sits on an old school desk. The desks are separate, like you're supposed to get the no-talking idea. In front of the closest one, I pulled out my Daily List Book. Usually no one's upstairs in the summer, but this time there was a person sitting nearby, a short person with a dark head. I was so surprised that I stopped dead and then slid sideways into my chair.

As I sat down, the person said, "Shoot!"

A girl. She sounded like she'd forgotten something. Either that or she was mad that I'd turned up. She pushed her chair back angrily and slap-slapped past my table, toward the stairs. Flip-flops. I looked up. She looked down. Neither one of us said a word. That's kind of unusual for Three Oaks, where everyone always says hello. Maybe we'd startled each other.

Here's what I saw: a round pink shirt, a plum-shaped chin, and hair in two pointy pigtails. The pigtails stood out like horns that had slipped down on either side of her head, one lower than the other.

Slap, whack, smack — rubber beach sandals on a marble staircase can sound like firecrackers.

After she left, I crossed off -Walk to Library. My pen suddenly burped out a small puddle of purple ink. I tried spreading out the extra with one finger, but that made it worse: Now I had a blob on a stick, or maybe a puff coming off a smoke bomb. My tidy list was getting messier by the second. Dangerously messy. Just like this summer.

I wondered if Firecracker Girl would be back, and why she was upset. What if she and Buckeye met and blew up at the same time, like a chemical reaction?

The thought made me smile, and then they both seemed less scary.

The Gas Gazette: Issue Five

A FREE NEWSPAPER ABOUT A MYSTERIOUS SOUL

~When I was young, my brother and I made a chemistry lab in the gardening shed. We had test tubes and burners and all kinds of other equipment. Our lab made some very bad smells.

~Once we dissolved real money, silver sixpences.

~I heard a story of a student who got tipsy with laughing gas and thought he could fly; that wasn't me, don't get any ideas.

~I was so serious about teaching myself chemistry whenever I was home that other students gave me the nickname Gas.

~When I was much older and had a bad stomach, I remembered that name.

~I think every name you've ever had stays with you, like the layers in a tree trunk or the skins on an onion. It becomes a part of you.

Who am I?

NEXT ISSUE TO COME.

FREE!

i spy

WHEN I TYPED in *BUCKEYE CHAMBERLAIN* that afternoon, my heart began thumpa-whumping. I knew it was kind of a sneaky thing to do, to look for information about a maybe-father I'd just met. But connecting the word *family* to Buckeye felt just plain wrong. I couldn't see that he was anything like us Chamberlains. I was just trying to be ready for whatever came next.

After counting the eighteen letters in his name, I took a deep breath and hit the ENTER button. There were lots of entries, but not one speck of information that fit.

Then I felt so sleepy after my night of worries, I put my head down on the computer and closed my eyes. Just for a second. Next thing I knew, Gumps was shaking my shoulder.

As I sat up, he squinted at the screen and saw Buckeye's name in the box. His eyebrows went up. Then he leaned down next to my ear and rumbled as quietly as he could, "Find anything?"

I shook my head. "I thought I might find his home or his job," I said, although I'm sure we both knew I was wondering about more than that. Things had happened so fast last night that my grandparents hadn't asked Buckeye where he'd been living all these years. And he hadn't told.

"Probably the same old nonsense. Drinking his way through life," my grandpa muttered.

Then I had a frightening thought: What if Buckeye Chamberlain had come back to Three Oaks because he wanted to stop? What would it be like if he decided to come home?

red

WALKING BACK FROM the library, Gumps and I were both quiet. When we passed the store, he tried the front door to be sure it was still locked. Then he walked around the back and did the same thing. This told me he had a pocketful of worry crumbs, too.

The only time we both looked up quickly was when a truck drove down Elm Street, going fast. It was headed in the direction of our house.

My grandpa muttered "Shoot," something he hardly ever says, and grabbed me by the shoulder. Weird, I'd heard two *shoot*s in one day. Gumps can't cover ground fast with that clanky leg, but we ran. When necessary, he shouted, "Curb!" or "Dip!"

"That Buckeye?" I panted.

"Dunno," he panted back. "Red. Looked like the same truck."

When we turned the corner, we saw a state police cruiser parked in our driveway but no red truck in sight. An officer was banging on our kitchen door.

blood and guts

WE GOT TO the steps just in time to hear the police-man introducing himself as Officer Nab, then asking Gam if she was Buckeye Chamberlain's mother.

"Yes, sir," she said. Her voice was as flat as old soda pop. "Zoomy, could you go upstairs and get my reading glasses for me?"

"*Now?*" I asked. I knew she probably didn't need them.

"Now," Gumps said firmly.

I walked as slowly as I could. I really wanted to hear. Why had they sent me away? That never happened.

I kind of shocked myself by wishing Buckeye had run into a tree or met some other bad end. I'd never known anyone who died, but it seemed like it would be a relief to all three of us. Bingo — gone! Then I thought about how violent car accidents were, and about blood and guts. Quickly crossing off that idea in my mind, I put lots of thick, purple *X*s on it. How had I imagined some-thing so nasty?

When I got back downstairs with the glasses, the officer was drinking iced tea at the kitchen table. After talking about the weather and what a good year it was going to be for tomatoes, he asked directions to Drier's Meat Market, which is an old family business just down the street from the store. They've been there since 1875 and are famous for their sausages, bratwurst, baloney, and hams. If he was thinking about Drier's, he couldn't have been there to report a death. He asked if it was true that Al Capone had bought meat there, and Gumps said yes. Gam wasn't saying much of anything.

As soon as Officer Nab drove away, I said, "So is Buckeye okay?" I tried to sound as though I wanted a happy answer.

There was a pause, and I knew my grandparents were looking at each other.

"Siddown, Zoomy," my grandpa said. "The state police are wondering if we know where Buckeye is. And whether he was in Flint last week. They asked what he was driving."

"Why?" My voice came out in a squeak.

"No idea. The officer didn't say." Gumps took off his baseball cap, itched his head with the rim, and put it on again. He sometimes does this when he's uncomfortable.

"Did you tell?" I was sitting in my chair now, and had just crossed off ~State Policeman Visits in my notebook.

"Of course." My grandpa clanked across the kitchen with the iced tea glasses and put them in the sink. "No idea about Flint, though. That's a sorry place these days. Highest unemployment rate in the country."

Gam was spreading macaroni and cheese into a casserole dish and sprinkling bread crumbs on top. "We didn't mention the box," she said, as if talking to herself.

"No," Gumps said slowly. "Think we should have?"

Gam turned around. "It just didn't feel right to add more trouble to a heaping plate. The trooper said Buckeye's had other run-ins. Misdemeanors, he called them."

"Whoa," I said, my mind darting around like mad. "Like what?"

"We didn't ask," she said.

"Why not?" I asked. "What if keeping the box makes us criminals, too?"

Gam spun away and started bing-bonging dishes around in a cupboard. Gumps sighed, a sigh big enough to blow things across the room.

"I hadn't exactly thought of it that way, Zoomy," he boomed. "Kin is kin. Around here you're innocent until proven guilty. Plus, we don't even know what the problem was. We'll keep that box in the garage for a few days. If Buckeye needs to take it, he will."

I stayed quiet. I somehow knew I'd said enough.

I thought about the Rule, the saying about treating other people the way you'd like to be treated. That's what my grandparents had just done.

I felt suddenly ashamed of my unkind thoughts, and tried to worry about Buckeye, too. But all I could see in my head was that sliced-up eyebrow and his prickly throat sliding up and down as he gulped water at the sink. That and his big hand grabbing my notebook.

The thought made me shiver.

a palindrome
with a stutter

"WHAT DID YOU say your name was?" Firecracker Girl's voice sounded loud.

"Zoomy." I was pretty sure her next question would be *What kind of name is that*. It wasn't.

"That's bizarre," she said. "Mine's Lorrol, spelled *L-O-R-R-O-L* instead of *L-A-U-R-E-L*. My mom's a ra-ra-rotten speller. She claims the spelling was on p-p-purpose, but anyway — it's good luck being a palindrome."

"Oh," I said.

"And don't say you like it," she added, as if I'd been picking a fight.

"Okay." I paid some attention to my computer.

Bizarre... I knew it meant kinda strange. It also sounded like city talk. Who *was* this girl? And what the heck was a palindrome?

Things were quiet for a few minutes on the second floor of the library. A train roared by outside, shaking the building. Silence again. I'd been doing a search on the emerald ash borer beetle, just to be sure I'd know if I found one — they're deadly for ash trees, and have been turning up in Michigan. Now I typed in *palindrome* instead. I found out it meant language you could read backward or forward.

We were both so still that when my stomach made a *gurgle-wurgle-urgle*, it sounded deafening. I crossed my arms in the middle of it, but it kept going. There's no stopping a stomach when it gets like that.

Lorrol's chair squeaked, and then she laughed. First I thought she was blowing her nose. The sound was closer to a sucked-in goose honk than a giggle.

"Sa-sa-sorry," she said. I realized she might be lucky, but she had a stutter. That somehow made me braver.

"That's okay," I said, wanting to laugh, too. If my grandpa had been there, he would've been asking how many piglets I'd swallowed whole.

I tried to change the subject. "Did you ever think of a palindrome like it was a horseshoe?" Why did I say *that*?

"Huh?" Lorrol said.

"I mean, good luck — two sides the same — that stuff," I said. I wasn't sure where to look, so I kept looking at the screen in front of me.

"What's up with those g-g-glasses?"

Whoa. She certainly didn't believe in hiding any questions.

"I have Pathological Myopia," I said, feeling a bit proud that I had some long words to say, too. I was kind of glad she'd asked. "I'm legally blind," I added.

"Ohhh," Lorrol said. "That's tough."

"I'm used to it," I said.

"Well, I like your glasses," she said. "I think they make you look really brainy. Are you?"

Whoa again. "I dunno," I said stupidly.

"Sha-sha-SHOOT!" Lorrol shouted, jumping to her feet. "I forgot again!" And off she went, her flip flops doing their *whap* routine on the stairs.

Firecracker Girl was a lucky palindrome with a stutter. But why was I thinking about luck these days? And why had the mean dent left by Buckeye's truck in the garden looked like a horseshoe?

I reached for my Daily List Book after Lorrol left, but didn't know what to write; if I crossed off her name, would that be unlucky?

The Gas Gazette: Issue Six

A FREE NEWSPAPER ABOUT A MYSTERIOUS SOUL

~My father wanted me to become a doctor, like him. I tried, but I couldn't stand seeing people in pain. In those days, if you had to have your arm cut off, they just did it. Doctors heard lots of screaming.

~I agreed to go to school in order to become a minister. At least I'd be able to take long walks in the country while I thought about sermons.

~Instead of doing all of my minister homework, I spent time talking with a naturalist at the university. I helped him collect the living specimens he was studying. I was great at capturing toads.

~Once I spotted a rare insect-eating plant in a wet, marshy area. I tried to use a long pole to vault expertly over a bad spot. I wanted to get there before some other students, and didn't do it right. I flew up in the air and was soon stuck on the top of the pole.

~Everyone laughed as I slid down, into the mud and muck. I got the plant.

~I had plenty of worried, insecure, embarrassing moments in my life. But I kept gathering and sorting.

~Determination counts.

Who am I?

NEXT ISSUE TO COME.

FREE!

dilly beans

THE NEXT DAY, I thought about Lorrol more than I did about Buckeye or chores. What was she doing in the library two afternoons in a row, and on the computers? Most local kids went to a day camp or helped their parents during the summer.

Summer is the busiest time for our family, and that's true for most people in Three Oaks. Folks are either growing things, making them, or selling them. Sometimes all three.

Each year, Gumps fertilizes and turns over the soil in the garden, Gam plants and prunes, and I water every morning and evening. I can't see where the water from the hose lands, but I know just how hard to make the spray, where to point it, and how long to hold it. I also do a ton of weeding.

I've found some awesome bugs when I'm down on my hands and knees, and because I'm so close I can witness a bunch of drama. Like people, some insects seem to want attention and some don't. Some are fearless and dress loud, and some are timid. Secretive. Some eat leaves in a tidy way, and some eat here and there, leaving a mess.

If I find a bug that is hurting one of our plants, I lure it carefully onto a leaf and leave it out in the grass. Behind the toolshed. I figure it'll be weeks before it gets back to where I found it, and maybe it'll get distracted meanwhile. Or go exploring. I only keep the dead ones.

Our vegetables are a big part of what we eat, and the garden fills up most of the backyard. I keep lists of what we've planted each spring, when each kind of plant comes up, when we harvest, and how much we get. This year we put in lettuce, parsley, basil, spinach, cabbage, cucumbers, summer squash, zucchini, eggplant, peppers, peas, beets, four kinds of tomatoes, three kinds of beans, and two kinds of pumpkins. Gam freezes a lot of veggies right away, and makes pickles and soups and casseroles and breads out of others. I help her with that by washing and chopping so that we don't mix in bugs or dirt. When we get a particularly good crop, Gumps shouts proudly that God Loves Dilly Beans — spicy, pickled green beans, his favorite snack — and Gam shushes him.

While I helped my grandma tie up the climbing beans that day, I wondered if Lorrol liked dilly beans. And I wondered why she was always alone.

don't ask, can't tell

HERE'S MY USUAL summer routine: In the mornings I -help Gam with laundry or the garden or cooking, and in the afternoons I either -go to the store to help Gumps and keep him company, or -go to the library.

We hardly ever visit Lake Michigan, which is about twenty minutes away by car. That's because we're doing all these jobs. Plus, we aren't sand fleas, as my grandpa says. None of us learned how to swim or lie on the beach.

Michigan orchards turn out a lot of fruit, and Gam makes pies and jams from blueberries, strawberries, plums, cherries, peaches, pears, and apples. She's famous in town for her secret pie recipes. I know them all because I help her measure the ingredients, but I'll never tell. (Here's a hint: Think more about lemons and real maple syrup than about sugar from a bag.)

Summer folks love her cooking, so she sells as many pies and other things as she can make. Sometimes she swaps her apple tarts or plum-cranberry crumble for venison steaks in the fall, since Gumps doesn't go shooting anymore. She trades jars of jam for fresh eggs. She once swapped eight loaves of her pumpkin-walnut bread for a Christmas ham from the meat market.

Everybody local knows just about everybody else in Three Oaks, so trading food is easy because they also know who does a good job on what. Lots of people here grow their own backyard vegetables even if they have a regular-paying job, and some also set up a table and sell the surplus at a farmers' market on Elm Street — Saturdays from late spring to early fall. Mostly they sell to folks with houses close to Lake Michigan, people who drive inland to visit our one-street town and buy fresh food. My grandparents decided not to have a stand after I got big enough to help; that's because city people asked more about why I was looking so close at everything than they did about our veggies. Everyone seemed to have Eye Stories and some weren't too great to hear. My grandma kept saying, "Let's talk about tomatoes instead," but it didn't always work.

So we garden, cook, bake, and run the store. From July 1 to Labor Day, it's open seven days a week, just so Gumps won't miss any business. He doesn't like writing, so I keep a lot of lists for him. He finds things at yard and estate sales, and brings them back to sell. Sometimes it's a hodgepodge of stuff that needs to be sorted; I help him decide on what's junk and what's not. Most city folks don't know that he's happy to bargain. That's kind of a secret.

As Gumps says with a shrug when someone pays a whopping price for something he would have sold for less, "Don't ask, can't tell!" We never stick on dishonest prices; just a Visitor Price if we think someone out there will buy.

I wondered if Lorrol would think Chamberlain Antiques and Whatnots was cool, or as bizarre as my name. I imagined her saying, "You're so lucky!" as I handed her a horseshoe from our collection. I knew my grandpa wouldn't mind; old horseshoes are cheaper than a Sunday newspaper in our town.

Then I told myself not to be silly. She probably hated all old things. Anyone who made that much noise in a quiet place like our library was probably only interested in city stores where everything was new and life was loud.

But talk about loud! She was probably still laughing about the kid with superthick glasses and a squealing belly. Those gurgles could've won first place at a county fair.

If she was going to be at the library and on the computers this summer, we'd be alone again. A lot. I'd have to get braver. She clearly wasn't going to turn into a different kind of bug, like the hiding, shy kind. Like me.

Then I had an interesting thought. Unlike insects, people could decide to behave differently.

This time, I'd be the questions-starter.

we get curious

JUNE WAS BLOWING closer to July, and for a couple of days I was too busy to get back to the library. It was a windy, dry summer all over the Midwest, and when wind gusts across flat land, it doesn't like to stop. Not easily.

Wind equals extra work.

Stakes in the garden fell over, and it seemed like the crops were super-thirsty. Watering was tricky, because the spray blew where it wasn't supposed to go. A quilt flew clear off the clothesline one afternoon and squashed our new pea plants. We had to stand them back up and make little fences for them to lean on.

After lunch on the third day, I was clearing the plates when Gumps went out the kitchen door. The garage door slammed and then he clumped back in carrying a box I'd never seen before. Buckeye's box — it had to be. He clattered it down in the kitchen.

"Ash! Get that dirty thing off my table," Gam said.

We all looked at it. She was right, it did look like

it'd been traveling. The box was old, dark, and beat-up. It sure was sealed shut — first with tape, then clear plastic.

"Just want to open this and see if there's any diamonds inside." Grandpa Ash winked at me. "Or the *Mona Lisa*."

"Or Abe Lincoln's underpants!" I chimed in.

"Think we should?" Gam asked. "Is it ours to open?"

My grandpa shrugged. "Buckeye gave it to us. Been here for days now. Aren't you curious?"

My grandma's eyebrows went up and she turned away, like she did when she was interested but didn't want to let on.

"Come on, let's just look!" I said.

"Here, let's you and me take it back out to the garage," Gumps said. He picked up the box.

"Just open it on the floor," Gam said. You could tell she wanted to see, too.

"Nah, that's okay," my grandpa said, and flashed me a quick grin. "Doesn't belong in the kitchen, anyway. You're right, dear."

Gam had gotten out the big shears. "Ash Chamberlain, you would tease a woman to death!" she said, and reached for the box.

"Not so fast," Gumps said. "Thought you weren't interested."

"You boys are impossible," Gam said, smiling now. "I give up; open the silly thing on the table."

We did. We don't get that many surprise packages in our lives, so we were all a bit excited. Nothing like a small town for getting people curious.

inside the box

GUMPS SNIPPED AND pulled and soon all that plastic and tape was underfoot. The top opened easily, and I leaned in close. I saw an old blanket, a raspberry color, with worn places and broken threads.

"Silk," Gam said, running a finger along it. "Looks like a lap blanket, you know — something people used to have on the arm of a chair."

Gumps was already lifting it out.

"Careful, Ash, there may be something fragile in there," Gam warned.

"Ooh," he said, peeking into a fold. "I knew it! We're rich!"

Gam and I looked at each other and rolled our eyes.

Out came a small, square shape folded neatly in a pillowcase. Gumps unwrapped it and held up a worn notebook.

"Book," was all he said, sounding disappointed.

He handed it to me. I opened it slowly and turned a few pages. The writing was messy and the cursive was hard to read. Lots of it had been crossed off or scribbled on.

"Huh," I said. There was a paper label on the cover. "*Ga-la-pa-gos*," I read, sounding out the syllables. "*Ota-*something. *Lima*. What's a galapago? Some kind of fruit?"

Meanwhile, Gumps had carefully shaken out the blanket. There was nothing else in the box.

"Well," Gam said, "guess we don't have to worry about jewels. Probably a good thing. I don't know, Zoomy. Didn't you say 'lima,' too? Like the bean? Maybe it's a crop list, from some other part of the world. Should be fun to look at."

"Can I hold on to the notebook for later?" I asked.

"Why not?" Gumps said. "Box is worth something — they don't make those anymore. I'll take it in to the store."

"Take the blanket, too," Grandma Al said. "Maybe an antique-fabric person will see it. Looks too fragile to use."

"Zoomy, you coming with me this afternoon?" my grandpa asked.

I was still looking at the notebook. I kind of liked that no one had put his or her name on it. Maybe that meant it was like my Daily List Book — someone's private place for writing things down.

"Sure. Can I stop at the library first?" I put the notebook on the kitchen counter, near my pile of notebooks. "You can leave me, and I'll follow." I'd memorized the exact number of steps between the library and our store, and was allowed to walk that distance by myself.

I wanted to see if Lorrol was around.

a heavy hand

I CIRCLED THE computers on the second floor before sitting down at my usual desk. No Lorrol. No anyone.

I was surprised at how disappointed I was. I'd gotten myself all ready not to sound dumb, to ask her a bunch of questions before she could ask me any more. Plus, I was curious: Why was she always in such a hurry?

People worked all the time in Three Oaks, but they didn't usually *hurry*, especially in flip-flops.

Well, there was one good thing about being up there on my own: I could do more Buckeye investigating.

I typed *Flint, Michigan, newspapers* in the Search Box. Up popped the *Flint Journal*. This was a daily paper, which must mean lots of news. Whoa. I didn't know anything about Flint, only that it was one of the auto manufacturing places that had a lot of unemployed people now. Every kid in Michigan knew about the auto plants closing.

I sucked in air and blew it out hard, just like Grandpa

Ash did that day in the kitchen. Then I typed in *crimes, Buckeye Chamberlain*.

And there it was:

Flint Resident Suspect in Auto Theft

A red Ford pickup was stolen from outside Lonny's Steak House on Wednesday evening. The suspect is Buckeye Chamberlain, age 31, of Flint, formerly of Three Oaks. Mr. Chamberlain is an unemployed General Motors line worker who was laid off two months ago. The truck owner is an antiques dealer who requested anonymity.

The owner had entered the restaurant after parking the truck behind the building. He said he then saw local news of interest on the TV, and decided to eat at the bar. Mr. Chamberlain was the only other customer. A regular at the bar, Mr. Chamberlain was reportedly drinking heavily, and left the premises first. He had just informed the vehicle owner that he'd recently lost his apartment and even his car, but he would survive: He wasn't a "quitter." The bartender was able to identify him for the police.

When the owner left minutes later, the truck was gone. Mr. Chamberlain was not seen anywhere in the vicinity.

Anyone who has information on either the truck or Buckeye Chamberlain is requested to phone the Michigan State Police hotline.

A thousand jumping jacks would be an understatement for what my brain was doing.

I stared at the screen, my thoughts bouncing up and down. So Buckeye's truck was probably the stolen one. And what about the box? It must be valuable in some way. Otherwise, why would an antiques dealer —

Just then, a heavy hand clapped me on the shoulder.

old sauerkraut

I KNEW WITHOUT even turning my head that it wasn't Gumps. His hand always felt kind. This hand felt hard.

And then I smelled that old bandage smell, like something damp and unclean.

My heart leaped up into my ears. It was beating so fast I could hardly hear.

"Hi, runt," Buckeye said. "Good timing. All on your lonesome, huh?"

I swallowed hard. I wanted to turn off the computer screen, but instead I was suddenly tapping my chin. *Uh* - tap! *Oh* - tap! *Uh* - tap! *Oh* - tap! Maybe if I didn't move, Buckeye would go away, like an angry wasp. Gam had taught me never to let a wasp know you're afraid.

The closest help was probably down that long flight of marble stairs. As if he read my mind, Buckeye snarled, "No one's up here, and no one downstairs can hear us, kid." He grabbed a chair and sat down right next to me.

I put on my glasses — I'd taken them off for close

reading. Now I could see Buckeye's grimy hand and a pair of pants that looked as if they needed to go through the wash five or ten times. And there was his knee, poking through a hole.

He was leaning forward, reading the article. I studied the dirt under his fingernails and the way his hand trembled. His knuckles were dry and cracked. He sat back and snorted.

"Well, whadda you know? I'm famous. Busy doing a little background check, huh? Trying to get me in trouble?"

I managed to shake my head right away, but I was still tapping. I wanted to tell him about the policeman's visit, but no voice came out.

"Planning on turning me in, huh?"

I tried desperately to shake my head no, but by then I hardly knew what was doing what.

Buckeye snorted. "You *are* a weirdo, aren't you? Well, no *worries* — I'm not about to be caught." He was talking in my ear, and his breath smelled nasty, like old sauerkraut. "And if you tell anyone you saw me, you're as good as *gone*. Hey, you're just an *ac*cident with an in*visi*ble name — easy to clean up an accident. And if you want my parents to stay *sssaaaafe,*" he hissed, "you'll keep this little visit to your*self.*"

When I didn't say anything and just kept tapping, he hit me on the shoulder. That was the best thing he could've done. Suddenly my feet were up and running toward the top of the stairs, and somehow they took me with them. A string of bad words came from behind me, and then a chair turned over.

I'm not sure what happened next. My hand reached for the railing but only grabbed air, and then everything hurt: I was sliding and rolling downward, light-dark-light-dark-*thump-thump*-Ouch. I was at the bottom.

Footsteps hurried in from the next room and then the librarian, Mrs. Cloozer, was fussing over me. She offered a paper cup of water and asked what happened. I didn't say, and she didn't mind. My glasses were bent but not broken, so I left them on. It seemed like my eyes still worked. She called Gumps at the store, then she told me he was on his way.

"Is anyone upstairs?" I asked Mrs. Cloozer.

Orange curls bobbed cheerfully when she shook her head. "I don't think so." Then she smiled. "OH, I know what frightened you! You poor dear! There's a trapped sparrow up there, and sometimes it flaps around. I'm so sorry I didn't warn you — I feel dreadful."

I tried to smile back, but don't know what my face did.

A sparrow. I knew the building must have back doors and stairwells, and Buckeye probably knew all the secrets. Just from growing up in Three Oaks. He'd probably been that kind of kid, always sneaking around.

By the time Gumps puffed in the door, I was standing up. I didn't have to say a word. Mrs. Cloozer explained all about the sparrow and my fall.

My grandpa put his big hand on my shoulder, and in comparison to Buckeye's, it felt like night and day. Even his skin had caring in it.

"We're headed home, Zoomy" was all he said.

As we walked, Buckeye's hissing words burned like my freshly scraped elbow. *Weirdo* — the word hurt. My grandparents would be furious if they knew what Buckeye had said to me, especially the part about cleaning up an accident with an invisible name.

But what if he meant what he'd said? And then the threat about Gumps and Gam. *As long as you want my parents to stay safe . . .*

I didn't dare tell about seeing him.

What - tap! *If* - tap! *What* - tap! *If* - tap!

There was nothing to do but hurry along side by side as I chin-tapped clear down Elm Street, past one store after another, and right up to the kitchen door.

I'm not sure who was happier to get home, Gumps or me.

a snowball

EVEN WHEN I was safely seated at the kitchen table, the Deeps were everywhere. I felt as if someone had dropped me into a bathtub filled with cold water, or taken away my glasses and told me to play hide-and-seek with a maniac.

My grandparents understand a lot, and I could tell from how quiet they were that they knew I was struggling with a mountain of worry crumbs.

Gam washed off my elbow and worked on my glasses until they were straight again. She asked me if I could still see okay, and I nodded.

Finally she said, very softly, "Was it really a sparrow?"

I wanted to tell them the truth so badly that the rest of me told them the truth. I was tapping and my mouth was all wobbly and my eyes were a mess.

"Nothin' to do with Buckeye now, was it?" Gumps thundered.

Luckily, Gam hugged me right then, and no one could see my face. The truth was squished against some soft part of her body. The secret was getting heavier by the second. It felt like a snowball rolled in wet snow. Pretty soon it'd be too heavy to lift.

Both grandparents were waiting for an answer. Even the breeze coming in the window stopped.

Then I remembered the article. I sat up and blew my nose. Suddenly the Deeps felt a little less scary. Here was something I could tell.

"*Sort of* to do with Buckeye," I blurted. "I found a Flint newspaper report on the computer. About the truck being stolen. Buckeye's name is in it. He's a suspect."

Gam sighed, but her voice was more puzzled than surprised. "Oh-dear-oh-dear. So it surprised you —" she began, as if the news wasn't as important as my fall. That kinda made my scrapes feel better.

Gumps interrupted. "What else?"

I told about the antiques dealer who wanted his name kept out of the article, the restaurant with the truck parked outside, and the news about Buckeye being unemployed and homeless. Then I mentioned the part that asked anyone with information to call the police.

"No need for that," my grandpa growled. "We don't

know any more than what we reported a couple of days ago, and we still have no idea where he is."

But I do, I was thinking. *I do.*

Dinner was quiet that night. I guess we were all too distracted by Deeps and worry crumbs to do much talking.

Halfway through dessert, Gam tapped Gumps on the arm. "Better leave that blanket in the box for now. Don't sell either one."

"I know. They're at the store, but I'll stick 'em in a corner."

"Can I still look at the old notebook?" I asked.

"Don't think there's any harm in looking as long as we can hand it over to the police if needed," Gam said slowly.

"Fine," Gumps grunted.

Right then, I don't think any one of us felt like we could see quite enough. That's unusual in a household where Life is always a blessing.

*X*s

I TOOK THE notebook up to bed with me that night. Maybe a quick look at this old thing would get me thinking about less scary stuff than Buckeye.

The cover was red leather, and the label on the front had only three words, written vertically like a list.

I put my nose against the label. Mmm, it had a welcoming, musty smell.

After *Galapagos* came *Otaheili*. Or was it *Otaheite*? The handwriting was tough. And then the third word, *Lima*.

I opened the notebook. Everything on the inside front cover was crossed off but the word *Benchuca*, which was circled. On the left side was a date: *August 4th, 1835*.

I'd seen published books that were this age in cartons of yard-sale stuff, but never a notebook. As far as I could tell, ancient books weren't too valuable, at least not the ones we had in the store. Most were by authors no one read anymore. Plus, chunks had fallen out or they had mildew and silverfish.

On the first page, I saw what looked like a list, but it

was crossed off with a big, wiggly X. Whoa, this person was writing so quickly that a lot of the letters were flat, as if they'd fallen down. Was that *Pacaguas*? Then, *19th of January*. That was clear, and, at the bottom, a scrawled *1826*.

I turned the page. These were sentences, not a list, but again x-ed out. I could only read *Started for* and then *Hills all soft* two lines later. Halfway down the page was the word *matter*. Two lines later, *very soft* and *which*.

I yawned.

There's comfort in faded, everyday words, thoughts written a long time ago by someone who might've had rough moments, too. Like me. This notebook keeper had probably survived a bunch of surprises and lived to tell about it.

I picked up my Daily List Book and wrote -No More Dragons for Today. I was thinking about my old friend Harold, the one with the purple crayon. He'd invented his dragon, but I had a real one: Buckeye.

I crossed off my last entry about ten times, paused, and put a big X over the day's list. Closing my notebook, I put it on the floor next to my bed and placed the old notebook carefully on top of it.

Like Harold, I dropped my purple pen and slept.

new face in town

"PUNK!" PLAYER FOUR muttered. The thought of that drunk driving his new truck was awful, and the reality of the box inside it was horrifying. The player felt as though he'd been offered the chance of a lifetime, only to have it snatched away. Stolen.

"If it's the last thing I do," he added, grinding his teeth.

Knowing the police were only after a missing truck and not a truck plus some valuable object, he decided to start investigating on his own. He was a small-time antiques dealer, at least some of the time; this much was true. He'd misled a few customers but had never been caught. However, having decided that he wouldn't hand over the mysterious treasure he'd been delivering, he didn't like having this object taken by someone else. Not one bit. After all, he'd been guarding a secret, and some secrets should pay.

He bump-bumped over the railroad tracks in Three Oaks late on a summer afternoon. He'd seen the name of the town in the Flint Journal *report. Looking around, he scratched his head.*

"Well, I'll be," he growled.

He parked his rental car on the main street and turned off the engine. A giant, old-fashioned clock hung on the front of the public library, but no one was around to need the time. Birds were singing. The street was clean, and no stores were boarded up. An American flag flapped lazily in the breeze.

One kid, a little guy with crazy-thick glasses, crossed the street next to an old codger with a limp and a baseball cap. They went into the library.

"America fifty years ago," the player marveled to himself. "I wonder if there's any crime?"

soil

I WAS READY this time. I'd find out what Firecracker Girl was doing in Three Oaks before she had a chance to start in with the questions again. I knew from experience that if you give a beetle a poke, even a brave one, it hesitates.

Gam had called Mrs. Cloozer that morning and had asked her to move the computers downstairs to the main floor.

"Wouldn't that be better in terms of supervision?" I heard her ask sweetly. "Oh, you have? Aren't you something!"

When Gumps and I stepped through the library doors that afternoon, he boomed, "Well, much better."

"What?" I asked.

"Right over there," he gestured. "All set up."

I followed the direction of his arm past Mrs. Cloozer's desk, called out "Thanks!" and gave a quick wave in case she was nearby, then walked to the other side of the room. Fourteen paces away, I found all the desks and computers that had been upstairs. To my great relief, Firecracker Girl wasn't there. I didn't want her to think I couldn't go to the library on my own; after all, I'd been traveling a full block on Elm Street by myself ever since I'd turned twelve.

"I'll be over to the store and back for you at four, how's that?" Gumps had followed me partway across the room. "Hey, get the rhyme?" he chuckled.

I waved again. "I'll come over before that; just want to do some research," I said quickly.

"Sure you do," he trumpeted. Then Gumps paused, and I heard him blow a large puff of air.

"No worries, not that kind," I called. Why had I said *no worries* — those were Buckeye's words. Suddenly my hand felt trembly, and I wondered in a flash if you were always connected to a blood relative even if you didn't want to be. Or if you always inherited, even if you didn't want what you got.

"Good," my grandpa said. "Some soil is better left unturned." That was what he and Gam always said when it was time to get my nose out of something they didn't think was a good idea.

"No problem, see you in a bit," I said, and sat down at the closest computer. *Soil* was the right word, and I was happy not to turn it.

brain boy meets
firecracker girl

AFTER GUMPS LEFT, the library was quiet. I felt safe in this corner, knowing Mrs. Cloozer could see me. There was no way Buckeye would pop out of a back stairwell here — the computers were set up in their own little area, boxed in on three sides by tall, wooden shelving.

I started by typing *galapagos* into the Search Box.

Nope, not a fruit. A place. In the online dictionary, I read that it was "an archipelago of volcanic islands. . . ." I stopped — what the heck was an archipelago? Anyway, I learned that the Galápagos Islands are sometimes spelled the Spanish way, with the slanty accent over the second *a*, and sometimes not — but they're always pronounced ga-LA-pa-gos. Nineteen islands in the Pacific Ocean, with the equator running right through them. Famous for unusual wildlife. Part of the South American country of Ecuador, main language Spanish . . . blah, blah, Charles Darwin stopped there while traveling on a ship called the *Beagle*. Weird, a boat named after a small dog. Then the dictionary said something about Darwin's theory. I knew almost nothing about it, only that he believed humans and monkeys were somehow related.

I smelled coconut candy and then a voice said, "I knew it! Reading science for f-f-fun! I'm calling you Brain Boy!"

"Was not!" was the first thing out of my mouth. Drat! Nothing wrong with science, but that wasn't what I was doing, and what was she doing spying on me, anyway?

I'd promised myself I'd be the first to ask a question.

"Why're you here?" I blurted. This didn't come out quite as I'd planned. It didn't sound too friendly.

Lorrol backed away, her hands in the air. "No p-p-problem!"

"Wait, that isn't what I meant," I bumbled on. "I just thought it was unusual that you're doing stuff on the computers and you're in the library so much."

"Oh, I s-s-see! Girls in your town don't hang out on the computers, huh?"

"No, that isn't what I meant!" I was starting to get a tiny bit mad. "No wonder you're Firecracker Girl!" The words were out before I knew it.

Lorrol paused. Then she started in on that same honking laugh. It was such a crazy sound that I couldn't help smiling. "I love that name!" she said in between honks. "Brain Boy meets Firecracker Girl!"

"It was just that you were in such a hurry and your flip-flops were so loud on the stairs," I explained.

"No, it's perfect for me," Lorrol said, her voice grinning. "I'm always exploding in a dangerous way. It's one of my greatest assets."

I believed it. But what the heck was an asset? Couldn't be what it sounded like. And where had her stutter gone?

i fly

A LOT CAN happen in a few minutes.

Yesterday's short visit with Buckeye had made my stomach crash to my toes. I felt like I'd fallen into a pit and might never get out. Today, ten minutes in the same building felt like heaven. Like I'd suddenly realized I could fly.

Somehow, maybe because I'd gotten mad and called her Firecracker Girl, Lorrol and I were talking. And it was ~easy and ~oddly comfortable. Nothing like this had ever happened to me before.

I told her I was from Three Oaks, and that I'd always lived with my grandparents.

She told me that she was eleven and a half and lived with her mom, Esther, who was a registered nurse at a private school in Detroit. They had a second-floor apartment nearby, and Lorrol went to the school for free. A summer in Three Oaks happened only because her mom found a part-time job as the nurse at a nearby day camp, and Lorrol was in the library because she hated the camp and told her mom she'd write and read instead. She explained to me that she was planning to be one of the best investigative reporters in the country. Then she explained that that meant uncovering big news and never being bored.

Next she told me her mom was a Russian Jew and her dad was *probably* from Jamaica, an island in the West Indies. Her mom wasn't quite sure, and her dad wasn't around to ask.

"Our last name is Shein, which is my mom's name," she said. "It's spelled *E-I* but pronounced like the *E* jumped to the end."

I imagined a leaping *E*, which seemed just right. Then I told Lorrol about my last name and my beginning on the kitchen steps and my mom, Abelina. I talked about never meeting her, and not knowing what her last name was or if she was really and truly my mom.

"Hey, that makes two of us!" Lorrol beamed. "We belong to the Unknown Parent Club, or U.P.C. for short."

She was sitting right next to me now, at a neighboring computer. I noticed the backs of our hands were just about the same color.

"Yeah," I said.

"So where's your dad?" she asked.

"I don't know," I said truthfully. I wanted to add, *It doesn't matter*, but Lorrol had already moved on.

"I think NOT growing up with two parents is the best, don't you?" she asked. "Kids like us are much more capable, that's my conclusion. They don't expect everything to just happen; they learn how to make their own luck. The U.P.C. is the most mysterious and intriguing kind of family club — that's what my mom always says."

Lorrol sure used a lot of big words. I guess she did like to read. The list to look up was now: -Archipelago, -Asset, -Capable, and -Intriguing. Wait, *intriguing* had something to do with hidden stuff. That I knew.

I liked the idea of making my own luck, and thought about the horseshoes at the store. It was funny she'd mentioned luck.

"Want to visit our family business?" I asked. "We specialize in mysteries and secrets."

I startled myself by saying that; I'd never thought of our store that way. Firecracker Girl was taking us somewhere — and even though I had no list that fit, the *us* felt fine.

Sometimes there's no turning back.

The Gas Gazette: Issue Seven

A FREE NEWSPAPER ABOUT A MYSTERIOUS SOUL

~After university, I was offered a job as a naturalist on an old sailing ship called a brig, doing "collection, observing & noting." It was my dream job. Plus, I would travel to faraway places.

~I was told the trip would take a few years and we would go around the world, so this was a bi-i-ig deal. My packing lists included everything from specimen jars and geological hammers and compasses to extra breeches and slippers and boots.

~My girlfriend was sad when she heard I was going, and my sisters fussed over me a lot. Both things were hard. The ship couldn't leave on time because of high winds, and waiting was agony. I got anxious, and my heart beat so wildly I didn't know if it would explode.

~A sailor fell overboard and drowned before we even left. I worried about dying. I thought about my family and friends and wondered if this was all crazy, but it was too late not to go. I would look like a fraidy-cat.

I ended my letters with "God bless you" and "Remember me," in case I never came home.

~I had to sleep in a hammock, in a tiny cabin with another guy. We could barely turn around. I slept over a table and two feet beneath the ceiling. I didn't know at first that the only safe way to get into a hammock is bottom first.

Who am I?

Have you ever slept in a hammock or been anxious about a trip?

NEXT ISSUE TO COME.

FREE!

christmas in june

LORROL SAID YES to visiting the store, and sounded just as excited as I was. But by then it was almost three o'clock, and her mom was about to pick her up out front. Whenever she was late, she explained, she had to pay her mom a dime. Suddenly I understood the flip-flops smacking on the stairs.

Her mom took her for a long bike ride every afternoon. "She's ruthless!" Lorrol sighed, as if it was a good thing. "On our ride a few days ago, I thought my head would blow right off my neck. And last week it rained so hard I almost drowned. She'll kill me with exercise, and then she'll be sorry."

After the ride, they always made either chocolate milk shakes or cocoa. They had a hot plate, a small refrigerator, and a blender in the room they'd rented on a farm down the road. Lorrol said her mom loved not having to cook.

I told Lorrol about my porch bike. "Very smart," she agreed. She said she'd give anything to have a bike she could ride while she was reading a book. "You are so lucky," she added. "I don't think my mom would let me have one of those."

Lorrol was like Christmas happening in June — I had that same can't-wait, what-if feeling inside. Like anything was possible.

At dinner I told my grandparents about meeting a kid today. I explained that she was in Three Oaks for the summer, and liked to be at the library while her mom was at work. "She's big on reading and writing," I explained.

Everyone stopped chewing when I said *she's*.

"That's nice, Zoomy," Gam said.

"What's her name?" Gumps boomed.

"Lorrol Shein," I said. "Like the sun, but spelled different. And by the way, what's an 'asset'? And what does 'capable' mean?"

"Hmm, lovely name," Gam said, and I knew my grandparents were trying not to sound too pleased. "I think an asset is something good. Valuable. And *capable* describes a person who can do lots of things."

"Sounds right," I said. "Pass the mashed potatoes, please." I didn't want to get too enthusiastic — that'd be carving the pumpkin before it's off the vine, as Gumps says. What if Lorrol turned out to be rotten, like her mom's spelling?

I smiled. Somehow, I wasn't too worried.

"She's a city kid and I don't think she's ever seen a place like the store," I said. "Can I bring her over one day?"

"Of course," Gumps said, and I could hear a grin. "What —" he began, then barked, "Ow, what's that for?"

"Finishing your spinach and minding your own business," Gam said.

I grinned. My grandma sure was a smart one. And Firecracker Girl was one hundred percent right about it being a lucky thing to be a member of the U.P. Club. My grandparents were the best.

I'd always thought that was true. I'd just never known it was an *asset*.

I said the word aloud as I was drying the dishes. Gam pretended she hadn't heard.

a simpler world

NOT SEEING A hotel of any kind, Player Four had asked at the gas station and been told that Mrs. Gander rented rooms. He drove across the tracks on Elm and parked in front of her house. There was no sign outside; his was the only car on that stretch of street. The front door was open.

Vintage clothing and a web of beaded crystal necklaces filled the living room. Her house smelled like his grandmother's in Indiana — furniture polish, scented soap, and fresh muffins. RING BELL IF YOU NEED ME, a small sign read. He rang the bell.

His room upstairs had no air conditioner but an ancient sleigh bed, lots of books, a once-elegant velvet sofa, and an old desk. Plus, the best part, a screened porch of its own looking into a pine tree and out on the street. The porch had a table and two chairs.

That evening he walked around the town. There was an old cannon in a park with a gazebo, a place to buy ice-cream cones, a hardware store, a pharmacy, a gun shop, and — yes! — Chamberlain Antiques and Whatnots. The name in the paper had been Buckeye Chamberlain — he had the correct town, all right.

Player Four tried the door. It was locked. He peered in the window. The place was a rat's nest of junk, with a few old dressers and rockers here and there. Hardly what he'd call real antiques.

He sat down on a nearby bench and looked up. A gentle, pale yellow moon appeared and disappeared in puffy clouds. The sky was a deepening purple, and suddenly he felt as though he were tumbling back in time. Was it that the scene reminded him of an illustration in a book he'd had as a kid? He closed his eyes, listening for a moment to the distant whistle of the approaching train and the brum-brum of summer insects. So much green. So much sky.

He hardly remembered visiting his grandma, but knew she'd also lived in a quiet town surrounded by fields. Growing up in Detroit, it was a world he'd only glimpsed as a kid.

The train roared by, its lighted windows come and gone in seconds. Silence resettled on the street. For a moment, the man sitting on the bench didn't care about the stolen box, or his truck.

On the way back to his room, he passed an elderly couple out for an evening walk. They nodded and smiled. "Nice evening," the man said.

"Lovely," the player heard himself reply.

The door to Mrs. Gander's house was still ajar; the old lady, watching TV in a pink dressing gown and slippers, explained that she rarely bothered with locking. Did he want her to bolt it? He shook his head.

Brushing his teeth that night, Player Four felt sad. Why wasn't he living in a simpler place like this? In a world where people said what they meant and trusted one another?

Drying his face with a towel, he told himself not to be such a mush; he'd find the punk's family, and certainly the treasure.

It'd be like taking candy from a baby.

nine words

THAT NIGHT I kept turning pages. Carefully. As I puzzled out words, I wondered if the person who wrote in the notebook had ever had a day like the one I'd just had — one that felt like a gift, a clear beam of light. The Deeps weren't endlessly deep anymore.

This long-ago person seemed like someone who'd had confusions also; a lot of the handwriting was unclear or scratchy. Sometimes there was a list running on and on, sometimes just word after word and an occasional mark like a comma or period. Almost every page was crossed out with a big, shaky X.

I thought of Grandma Al's tidy, looping grocery lists. Her writing was so strong and clear it looked almost like the cursive words in my spelling book. Even my Daily List Book was neater than this. A lot neater.

The word *Galapagos* on the cover label had no little mark over the second *a*. I'd looked up Otaheite and found it was a name for what's now the island of Tahiti, and Lima was a city in Peru. This person was traveling.

Inside, the short words were easiest to decipher: *all*, *before*, *which*, *is*. And then I found this list: *Wednesday, —* *Sea, Shells, Thermometer*, followed by numbers.

Next I picked out *salt mine*, and then *earthquake*.

On the following page, I read nine shocking words. I read them again and then once more, trying to give my brain time to catch up.

The Beagle called in on the 23rd of April.

no telling

THE *BEAGLE*.

Wasn't that the name of Charles Darwin's boat? How many *Beagle*s could there be? The words were crossed off this time with parallel, slanted lines.

There was so much I needed to find out. Like, what year was Darwin on the ship? What kind of stuff was he doing? Where did they go? And what was "called in" if there were no telephones?

What if I was holding a notebook kept by someone who traveled at the same time as Darwin, a person who maybe stopped on a nearby boat to get fresh water and supplies?

Maybe it was even someone who'd met Charles Darwin! Maybe Darwin had told him something special, and that's why this notebook was saved. Maybe it was important because of that one, sparkling moment.

My hands were shaking and my heart was bumpa-whumping like I'd just bicycled for about an hour. At top speed.

I couldn't wait for tomorrow.

I couldn't wait to tell Lorrol.

And then I did something odd, maybe just because I felt like the notebook shouldn't be lying around in the open: I wrapped it carefully in one of my T-shirts and put it in the Danger Box, the small fruit crate where I keep my collection of old firecracker cases, smoke bomb wrappers, and shotgun shells picked up from the town park and anyplace else on the day after the Fourth of July. Because my grandparents aren't wild about the collection, I keep it under my bed. It's not exactly hidden, just out of sight.

After the notebook was safely stored away, I reached for my Daily List Book. Since I always end each day with a *no* somewhere in the last entry, I wrote, -No Telling What I'll Find Out Tomorrow!!!!!

I went to sleep picturing the Search Box on the computer. The Search Box, and Lorrol and me looking at it. Side by side. Plus that coconut smell.

The words *no telling* washed back and forth in my head like waves hitting a beach. Like a beach seen on a voyage.

No telling, no telling, no telling . . .

The Gas Gazette: Issue Eight

A FREE NEWSPAPER ABOUT A MYSTERIOUS SOUL

~If you've never been seasick, let me tell you: It's a nightmare. I got so sick, right away, that all I could do was lie in my hammock and gag and groan. I had nothing but "dark & gloomy thoughts." I lived on dry biscuits and raisins.

~The weather got better as we headed south. The waves weren't as choppy and my stomach felt more normal. We stopped in the Cape Verde Islands, 300 miles from the coast of Africa, and I was thrilled to get off the boat and do some hiking and collecting. Everything was new and exciting. I was told to carry a gun, but no islanders attacked us.

~I was "overwhelmed" when I first saw tropical plants and creatures. I took notes and collected madly.

~Once back on the boat, we headed for the equator. Bang, I was sick again. I was "squeamish and uncomfortable" and felt as though I was being "stewed in . . . warm melted butter." I lay in the sticky-hot hammock, staring miserably at the dead creatures

I'd collected as specimens. My hammock wouldn't stop rocking.

~Being helpless in a strange place made me horribly homesick. It's hard not to panic when you feel rotten.

Who am I?

Have you ever had to throw up away from home?

NEXT ISSUE TO COME.

FREE!

seeing

I WOKE UP the next morning knowing something I hadn't realized the night before: *No telling* were the right words. I couldn't tell Lorrol about the notebook. Not until I'd told my grandparents. What if she told her mom, and her mom told someone else . . . and Buckeye overheard?

I couldn't forget: Buckeye had *stolen* this notebook. Maybe. At least, it seemed like it had come with the truck. And the truck was probably not his.

If I told my grandparents, and they decided the notebook had to go to the police because it might be valuable, would Buckeye think I'd told on him? If caught, he'd get in even more trouble.

And if not . . . would he then try to hurt my grandparents or me? Would he get even scarier and angrier?

I didn't dare. What if this was like a lineup of dominoes — if I tipped one over and then a whole bunch more went down?

Yup, the *Beagle* should stay a secret, at least for a while.

After getting dressed, I felt under my bed. Whew, the Danger Box was still there. As I hurried downstairs to breakfast, I began getting excited all over again about seeing Lorrol and looking at the Search Box together.

No reason we couldn't find out some stuff about Darwin's life. It was a perfect summer project, and was definitely investigative reporting.

I didn't like the idea of having to hide part of the truth from everyone, but I was caught between Buckeye and my grandparents.

No choice. Sneaky was the only possible thing to be. At least until I could see better what was going on . . . well, not *see*, but see what I could tell.

For someone with bad eyesight, I sure was seeing a lot.

a bug's life

I WAS DYING to get back to the library after the morning chores, but Gumps asked me to help him at the store.

At first I wanted to say *Can't it wait*, but then I pictured Lorrol sitting at the computer next to mine, wondering where I was. I smiled — *Brain Boy meets Firecracker Girl. Firecracker Girl misses Brain Boy*. Plus, this would give me a chance to dust off our collection of horseshoes before I brought Lorrol to the store.

"Gotta open early today," my grandpa boomed. "Mrs. Lister, the one on Pine Street, is bringing in two family quilts she wants to sell."

Gam made a clicking sound. "Really! That's too bad. Family quilts should stay family."

"Tough times, Al, old girl. Lotta people needing cash, and those quilts go like hotcakes with the Chicago folks." Gumps was already putting on his baseball cap, the one that said OLD COUNTS.

"Ready," I said.

"I'll bake," Gam said. "They've asked for more carrot cakes at the Green Door Dairy, and what's good for the belly is good for the button jar."

We say *button jar* instead of *piggy bank* — I guess because recycling buttons was the same as saving money in the old days, and the old days aren't too old in our household.

"Save me the icing bowl!" I called as I put on my sneakers.

"I will," my grandma said, and I could hear she was smiling.

"Lock that door," Gumps growled as we stepped outside.

"Yes, yes." Her voice floated through the window as if he'd said something silly, but we did hear the bolt thump into place.

He and I walked for a few minutes without talking, listening to the bugs whizz-trilling and the leaves shushing and the whole complicated mishmash of summer sounds. He leaned down and picked up something dark. I could see it coming closer in his palm.

"Whadda we have here?" he thundered. "Well, just a plain honest-to-goodness June bug. Want it?"

I nodded. I have a glass jar filled with dried bugs of

all kinds on the kitchen windowsill. Sometimes in the white Deeps of winter I pull them all out and line them up like soldiers. Soldiers in summer colors — up close, you can spot flashes of purple, green, yellow, red, and orange. Once in a while the three of us play Monopoly using my dried beetles for game pieces.

I took off my glasses and moved the dead beetle back and forth in front of my nose. He was perfect, with tattooed arms and pajama stripes down his back.

"It must be nice to have the life of a bug," I said. "No real worries."

"Hmph," Gumps said.

"All you do is make noises and walk and eat and hide from things that want to get you," I said.

"Doesn't sound too easy to me," my grandpa boomed. "I'd rather come downstairs and find blueberry muffins in the morning and an icing bowl in the afternoon. And I don't think that fella's looking forward to hot dogs on the grill tonight."

I smiled, and slipped the beetle into my T-shirt pocket. Now that I thought about it, Buckeye could squash me like a bug. Good thing I wasn't even smaller.

"You're right," I said.

Gumps nodded. "Dang right."

old counts

MRS. LISTER NEVER showed at the store, and I could tell my grandpa was a little disappointed. "Those old quilts are an easy sell in the front window," he muttered. "Come on, help me get prices on this box of plates. Came from a yard sale out north of the Hurley place."

Because my world is up close, I don't have a clear picture of what's in the countryside around Three Oaks aside from fields and trees. My grandparents describe where things are by talking about the location of people's houses, sheds, or barns — it's never about the roads. Sometimes it isn't even about the living owners. People call our house the Turner place, even though Gam's parents died a long time ago and she and Ash Baker Chamberlain have lived there forever.

"I hope I'm still in our house when I'm your age," I blurted out.

Gumps grinned. "Nice thought," he said. "Your grandma and I will be dried and propped up in the corner like a coupla corn-husk dolls, and you can charge admission."

I poked him then and he poked me back and we got to work. He dictated, and I wrote the labels, like: *Wedgewood, 1838, chipped — $4.00.*

I loved the store. Speaking of corn-husk dolls, it was kind of like the whole Baker-Turner-Chamberlain family was in there, even the ones who were long gone. Like history wasn't history anymore, at least in that one space; the past was still alive, and all around us.

I thought about the notebook in the Danger Box. I was itching to tell Gumps about it. He and I often made up stories about the odd things in the store . . . like, a certain mirror with roses on the frame must've belonged to a young girl with red cheeks and a green thumb, or a certain pair of fancy boots belonged to a man who only wore them to church and limped every time.

I knew Gumps and I could make up a great adventure to go with the old notebook; maybe a story about picking up shells when an earthquake struck, and suddenly the *Beagle* came into view and there was Charles Darwin shouting, "Are you okay?" from the deck, just as a huge wave hit. . . .

For some reason, the thought of a disaster made me think of Buckeye, and that squelched the story, at least for the moment.

"Hey!" Gumps was speaking. "You crossing the Alps? Head in the clouds! Give me that blue and white saucer."

"Sorry." I grinned.

It was quiet for a few minutes while Gumps and I sorted. The front door was wide open, but there was no need to keep an eye on it — we always heard a visitor.

The floors in our store were wood, and creaked loudly with every step. Even Gumps could hear them, and he said this worked better than any modern alarm system. He'd made paths through the mountains of stuff, mostly so I wouldn't trip. I had a torn-up red sofa in the back where I liked to read and look at things up close, and that's where I kept the lists of what my grandpa brought in from yard sales and, if I happened to be around, what he sold.

We weren't exactly sure how many treasures we had, because there were so many stacks, boxes, cabinets, and drawers. Once I found a dead mouse inside an old sugar bowl with the top on, but no sugar. We made up a Gam saying for that, something about All Sugar and No Spice

Kills Even the Fastest Mice. Some of my favorite things had been there for as long as I could remember — a stuffed crocodile with black pebbles for eyes, a giant bone sword with a wooden handle, a whole bunch of old postcards from places like Niagara Falls and New Orleans, a funeral bridle with black feathers from the horse-and-buggy days, an umbrella stand full of feather-bone whips, a hatbox filled with regular horseshoes as well as a worn Clydesdale horseshoe the size of my head — that's from one of those giant workhorses with hairy feet — and tons of old sewing boxes. Some of the things made you want to smile, and some felt kinda sad.

I opened the hatbox, turned a few horseshoes over, and picked a beautiful one for Lorrol. The edges were round with wear, and it wasn't too big. I wiped it off on the front of my T-shirt and left it on my sofa.

As we worked on the plates, Gumps sighed. "I'll tell you, Zoomy. I had a hard time sleeping last night. Things have been so quiet this year; I'm not sure we'll make it, with the taxes and all going up."

"What do you mean, 'make it'?"

My grandpa took off his hat, rubbed his head vigorously, and put it back on. "Old Counts, always will, but business over the last few years has just been slower and slower. Chicago folks aren't spending like they used to, and some aren't even coming to Three Oaks anymore. Everybody's hurting these days, and the numbers are way down. We're just lucky we own the store and our house. We'll always have something to eat and a place to sleep. At least that's the plan."

"Jeez," I said. There was a moment of silence.

"Didn't mean to scare you," my grandpa added.

From the quick scrape of his neck-whiskers against his shirt, I could hear Grandpa Ash looking at me. He said slowly, "We'll survive. And you're a go-getter kid."

Creeeak — pop! Pop! This wasn't someone familiar. I knew right away because my grandpa stood up and dusted off his knees. "Mornin'!" he said, and his tone of voice told me this was a guy.

I didn't hear the man reply, but I heard him walking slowly. *Creak, creak.* This meant he was looking at things.

"You Mr. Chamberlain?" the visitor asked. He had a funny *wa-wa* voice, like someone chewing on a hot marshmallow.

While Gumps walked around with the visitor, I got busy looking for my old science encyclopedia. Aha — under the sofa. It wasn't up to date, but it worked fine for researching beetles or plants, and also heredity and traits.

I needed more on Charles Darwin. Before I told Lorrol about my Investigative Research idea, I wanted a small head start. After all, she might already know a bunch about him.

Here's what I found out:

Charles Robert Darwin, born in 1809, died in 1882 . . . Almost a five-year voyage on the Beagle *. . . Published his revolutionary book* On the Origin of Species by Means of Natural Selection *in 1859 . . . His theory that all species of life evolved over time from common ancestors, because of natural selection, is now the foundation for all modern biology. . . .* What the heck were "species" and "common ancestors"? And what was "natural selection"?

I looked up as I realized the man was walking closer. I didn't feel like talking, so I took off my glasses and put my nose about two inches from the page. Sometimes it's useful to have my eyes; when I get that close to whatever I'm looking at, people don't usually want to interrupt.

The man walked past. Then I heard him stop.

"This box for sale?" he asked.

"Ah, no . . . just for storage," my grandpa replied.

I kept wagging my head back and forth, but stopped reading.

"Could I look inside?"

"I suppose so. But, ah . . . it's not for sale."

I heard the swish of fabric as the man lifted out the old blanket. He gave it a little shake.

"How about this?"

"Not today," Gumps said. "But I've got some nice English plates that just came in."

The man was walking back toward the front of the store now.

"Thanks" was all he said as he left. His voice had gone from city-friendly to hard as nails — and all in one word.

I closed the science encyclopedia.

"I wonder if we should call the police," Gumps said.

no police

I HAD TO think fast. I *believed* Buckeye, this was the problem. I believed he was capable of doing bad things to us. *Capable.* My shoulder still remembered his hard, mean hand.

"No police," I said. "Then we'd have to tell about where the box came from. Kin is kin," I added, feeling like a stinker. I didn't mean it the way my grandpa thought I did.

Gumps grunted. "Kind of you, boy. You're a good kid. But I didn't like the way that fellow recognized that old box. He was lookin' for something, that's for sure."

"You think?" I asked.

"I know."

"Huh," I said.

"What's in that old notebook, anyway?" My grandpa's voice was worried, which worried *me*.

"I think it's someone's travel book. No name but I saw an old date. I wanted to do some library research on it today, see if I can figure out what we got."

I didn't mention the *Beagle* — maybe because I was

afraid it would make the notebook sound too valuable. Then something hit me like a flash of lightning: *If I was careful, maybe I could rescue the store!* What if this notebook had belonged to someone close to Charles Darwin and it was worth a lot of money? The idea was dazzling.

But my grandparents . . . I knew they'd never agree to sell something stolen. But what if it wasn't . . . what if Buckeye had picked it up at a yard sale? And what if we called the police right now and they came for the notebook but didn't arrest Buckeye? What if he somehow found out I'd ratted on him? The thought made me breathless with dread.

"No police yet," I said. "Can I just have this afternoon?"

I heard Gumps scratching his head. "Just today," he said. "I don't like the idea of holding on to something hot."

"What if it's not? If it really *did* belong to Buckeye and he gave it to you, like he said?" I asked.

Clanking ahead of me toward the front door, my grandpa only grunted.

trapped

AFTER LOCKING UP the store, Gumps patted me on the back. "You're a spunky kid," he said. "But don't get carried away."

"I still need to go to the library," I said. "Can you walk me over after lunch?"

On the way home, neither of us said a word. I know we were both deep in worry crumbs.

Right then I hated hiding things and I hated secrets. And I realized something big: Secrets are only good when you want to keep them. When you're forced to keep them, they feel like they're eating you up inside. Like you can't escape. Like you're trapped. I thought of the mouse in the sugar bowl.

My stomach was churning, but I was strangely calm. It was almost as if I *couldn't* go jittery-splat. The list of people I had to keep secrets from was now every single person in my world.

One afternoon of trying to figure out what we had, that was all. Then I'd give the notebook back to my grandparents, they'd probably give it to the police, and who knows what would happen next. We'd keep the door locked.

-Go to Library, I thought, and crossed it off in my head. Picturing the x-ed-out line made things better. Then I thought of the shaky *X*s in the old notebook, and felt a surge of excitement.

What if I rescued our family? They'd be so proud of me once it was all over!

-One, -Afternoon: That was all. The thought was worth the weight of all these secrets.

As if he could hear me struggling, Gumps suddenly put a big hand on my shoulder. "You're a smart one," he said. Then he did something odd. He took off his Old Counts baseball hat and put it on my head.

It came down to the top of my glasses. "Thanks," I said.

I could picture the separate parts of myself moving along: First one blurry foot, then another, then my body, and my head in my grandpa's hat, surrounded by Deeps.

The Gas Gazette: Issue Nine

A FREE NEWSPAPER ABOUT A MYSTERIOUS SOUL

~I'll never forget first going ashore in Brazil. I thought I'd landed in heaven.

~I was dazzled by how dense and lush and beautiful everything was. Listening to a symphony of sounds — insects, birds, who knows what else — my heart was full. My mind was "a chaos of delight."

~I collected enough flowers "to make a florist go wild."

~One day I caught sixty-eight species of beetles. And I was "red-hot with Spiders," too. I never dreamed of all the glorious forms of life I was seeing.

~I was buzzing with excitement. I prepared tons of specimens to send back for examination.

~Sometimes I felt as though I was standing in a huge cathedral, with an oddly perfect mixture of singing and then silence, a grand and "universal stillness."

~Had I ever been so happy?

Who am I?

NEXT ISSUE TO COME.

FREE!

just am

LORROL PICKED THAT afternoon to explode.

As soon as I sat down, she slammed her hand on the table. Before she even said hi. I jumped.

"My mom is such a royal DORK!" she said. "Dork, dork, DORK!"

"How come?" I asked. I took off the baseball cap, suddenly realizing I might be next on the dork list.

"She wants me to start going to her camp. But I hate those kids! They've got chicken legs. And they're good at sports and like cold water. They all know each other. Plus, I'm BUSY. Here. In the library." Lorrol wriggled so fiercely in her chair that it skated along the floor, making a sound dangerously close to what happens if you eat too many dilly beans.

There was a pause, and then we both laughed. I mean, Lorrol honked. And suddenly the storm was over.

"If you had a big project, would she let you stay?" I asked.

"Maybe. Like what?"

I took a deep breath. "Like finding out everything about Charles Darwin. And a boat named the *Beagle*," I said.

"I knew it!" Lorrol crowed. "I saw the word *Galapagos* on your computer screen, and everybody knows that's where Darwin went."

They do? I thought.

"Maybe it could be investigative reporting, and you'll become an expert on this stuff," I suggested. "Then your mom would know you were doing something worthwhile." I was starting to turn into a big-time sneak. "You could take notes."

"You're brilliant, Zoomy!" I could hear Lorrol beaming. "So how come you're interested in Darwin?"

I shrugged. "Just am."

"Told you the name Brain Boy was a good one."

"Naw," I said, pleased but embarrassed. "I'm probably just stupid," I blurted. Little did she know *how* stupid: Playing games with what might be stolen property. But these weren't games, I reminded myself. This was my family. And the store. And I had one afternoon.

whoa

TWO HOURS LATER, Lorrol had taken every book on Darwin off the library shelves. We were barricaded in books. Meanwhile, I'd also been working the Search Box.

I found out a ton. Like, Darwin had been at the Galápagos Islands in 1835. And so had the *Beagle*; he'd traveled from December 27, 1831 to October 2, 1836. I wished madly that I could tell her about the notebook — she'd be so excited. Maybe soon.

I read that Darwin had been studying nature while on board the ship. He'd collected mostly rocks and fossils early on, then hundreds of plant and animal specimens. He did his best to preserve them, and sent everything back to England in crates. He studied and observed and recorded. One of the things he began puzzling over was where so many species came from, and how they became slightly or hugely different from one another — *species* meaning any group of living things that can reproduce. In those days, there was still a ton to be learned about how nature worked, and a ton no one understood.

Lorrol was sitting next to me, thumbing through the books.

"Did you learn about evolution in school?" I asked.

"Just a movie," she said. "Then I think we do more detail in eighth grade."

"So what does evolution mean? We haven't exactly gotten to it."

I was afraid Lorrol would make fun of me, but she didn't. She thought for a minute. "Actually, it's called the *theory* of evolution, which gets a lot of people confused. My teacher made a big point of explaining that evolution wasn't a theory meaning a *guess*. For scientists, a theory is an explanation backed up by so many facts that it must be right. You'd think experts would choose another word so as not to give the wrong idea.

"So here's what I remember: The theory of evolution is like a huge, tree-shaped jigsaw puzzle, a tree of life. Darwin sketched it out, and scientists of all kinds are still filling it in. I think it means seeing everything in the plant and animal worlds as being related, waaaay back. And the evidence is everywhere — in fossils, under microscopes, in our surroundings. The idea is that all of us came from a first spark of life and over a gillion-bazillion years, we *evolved*."

"You mean billions," I said.

"Yeah, exactly. Over an unbelievably long time we slowly, slowly became a bunch of different species. We kept changing and still are, because of survival of the fittest. Actually, Darwin called it natural selection, because natural happenings had a lot to do with who lived and who died — like climate, earthquakes or volcanoes, food supplies, disease, things like that. The *organisms* — isn't that a cool, sciencey word? — that could adapt and survive then passed along their, um, whatever —"

"Traits?" I wasn't feeling quite so dumb.

"Exactly. Others died out. Became extinct. It's all about change and luck. Or maybe it's probability."

I nodded. Did *probability* mean stuff that would probably happen? "Yeah, traits, survival, that's kinda what I thought," I said. "I have a science encyclopedia I look at sometimes."

Inside, I thought about survival of the fittest and shivered. Was Buckeye more fit than me and Gam and Gumps?

I took off my glasses, no longer caring if it made me look funny; I could read faster that way. Now we were both reading like maniacs. Lorrol was also scribbling things down on a pad of paper.

We both said "Whoa!" many times. You'd think we had a roomful of galloping horses. I forgot all about tricking Lorrol into helping me learn about Darwin; I was getting hooked. On my own.

"I never knew what kind of person Darwin was," Lorrol said. "He struggled with lots of things. He was an anxious, spacey kid who wasn't great at school. And a terrible speller, like my mom. Whoa, he had a stutter sometimes! Just like me when I first meet people. And guess what? He made lists all the time, just like you!"

I felt a *ping* of shock in my brain, like the first kernel of popcorn exploding in hot oil.

"Whoa," Lorrol went on, "he filled dozens of small notebooks, and kept them nearby all his life. Like he needed them. It sounds like he had to do things in special ways, or — yikes!"

I'd grabbed the book and was dragging it toward me, my nose now almost touching the page. I must've looked dangerous, because Lorrol sat back. I read like mad while Lorrol waited.

"Jittery-splat!" I shouted. I was so excited that a gob

of spit shot out and landed between us. I swiped around with my elbow.

"He'd get *what?*" Lorrol asked.

"Jittery-splat. It's what happens to me if too much is going on too fast and I get upset."

"Like me when I explode?"

"Yeah. There are slightly different kinds." I grinned at Lorrol and couldn't see her face perfectly, but I heard her grin back.

"Got it," she said. "Yours sounds less noisy than mine."

"Well, I dunno," I said. "But lists help me change gears. They're a tool. And it sounds like Darwin needed them, too! I never knew there was a famous person like that."

I kept reading. *Ping, ping* . . . the ideas were firing to right and left. "Listen to this!" I said. "He had a whole system, and used one kind of notebook for one thing, and one for another. And he carried something called 'field notebooks' when he left the *Beagle* to go exploring. That means he took notes wherever he was, and some were messy. Whoa, he also crossed everything off!" *PING!*

Then Lorrol said, "I'll bet everyone kept notebooks in those days, because that was the only way to record ideas. It's unusual now, but probably wasn't then."

"Yeah, maybe not," I said slowly. My mind was spinning wildly in the Deeps, sparks flying. Not only was Darwin a jittery guy like me, but he used lists and notebooks, also liked *X*s. . . . Was it even the tiniest bit possible that I really *did* have a Darwin notebook under my bed? Everything fit so perfectly!

"That's *crazy!*" Lorrol said, and I jumped. Had she just read my mind?

Busy with her book, she didn't look up. Suddenly I was tapping my chin, so I opened my Daily List Book and wrote ⌐Take Deep Breath. I did, blowing it out noisily like Gumps. I put *X*s on my line, and felt better. Crazy . . . *was* I crazy?

Yeah. Earth to Zoomy, as my grandparents sometimes said. Lorrol was right. Why would a Darwin notebook *ever* be found wrapped in an old blanket in a beat-up box in Michigan? I'd be more likely to see the *Beagle* sail out of the cornfield behind our house.

Lorrol went on, "Jeez, he had ten kids! He was nuts about them, and a few died — that's awful. He let his kids come in his study when he was working, and didn't get mad if they drew on valuable papers by mistake. He cared a lot about his wife. She was his best friend."

"Keep going," I said, sitting back in my chair. I was resting my popcorn brain, just for a minute.

"Okay, listen to this: He liked being home, and after going around the world on that voyage, he never left England again. Sometimes he'd walk and walk on a sandy path behind his house. Although he was sick a lot, he still kept working. And this: He tried in a not-selfish way to help other investigators who were also studying nature — he wrote and answered a ton of letters. He fessed up if he didn't know whether one of his ideas was right, and never wanted to hurt other people. A generous soul, that's what he was, and a *mensch*."

"What's that?" I asked.

"An all-around good kind of guy. A decent human being."

"And different," I added.

"It's all kind of amazing," Lorrol went on. "I mean, how could someone who was so gentle and shy stand to make such a giant fuss in the world? I'm reading here that his evolution theory got a ton of people all mad and upset, and some hated him. He *knew* that would happen.

He was such an unlikely guy to do what he did, you know?"

I nodded. "Yeah. A mysteriously quiet Firecracker Maker . . ."

I'm usually very aware of sounds around me, but that afternoon Lorrol and I might have been on the moon. We were in Darwin heaven, and oblivious.

Neither one of us noticed a man who wandered quietly back and forth between the stacks on either side of us. The floors in the library weren't creaky like those in the store. And he wasn't speaking.

He was listening.

a silent witness

"GAS! ISN'T THAT the best nickname?" I crowed.

"Awesome," Lorrol agreed. A second later she slammed the table with her book, making me duck. My head hit the computer screen.

"Ow!"

"I know what to do! Oh, sorry! Whoasie-doesie on high!" Lorrol was on her feet and clapping hands. "It's going to be the best mystery this town has seen in ages! It may spread around the world!"

"What, what?" My glasses were back on, partly to protect my face. Lorrol was all unidentified body parts, and now jumping.

"We can" — *thump!* — "put together a series of free newspapers" — *thud!* — "each maybe a page long, with details about Darwin's life, things not everyone would know. We won't use his name or the word *evolution*. He'll be an Unknown Person! But we can use his real words, like quotes" — *thump* — "from all that writing he did."

"Whoa." I grinned, and wished that I could blurt the news about the old notebook under my bed. Speaking of quotes! Keeping this secret was like sitting on a bunch of pinecones.

Lorrol had plopped down again but kept talking at top speed, her face about three inches from mine. "He's an inspiration to kids — to people of all ages! He had plenty of rough moments but didn't give up, you know?"

I nodded. "Yeah! He makes you feel like you don't have to know everything. You just have to keep trying."

"And stay curious," Lorrol added. "*Oooh*, we can leave these bulletins anyplace . . . in the library, like *oooo*! Stuck in between the pages of books! Or in a newspaper at the pharmacy! Or in between bike maps at the sandwich shop! But what should we call it?"

"How about the *Gas Gazette*?" I said, thinking of our local paper, the *South County Gazette*. "Gas is a great name."

That afternoon I got my first hug from Lorrol. My glasses slipped off and were ground into my chin, but it was worth it.

This was one whoa-rich, *ping*-crazy afternoon, and a definite life changer.

As our silent witness slipped out the library door, we were still chattering, filled to the brim with hope and ideas.

The Gas Gazette: Issue Ten

A FREE NEWSPAPER ABOUT A MYSTERIOUS SOUL

~I hiked through the rain forest, carrying my note-books and gun. I saw wonders in this "gold mine" every day — iridescent insects and birds, giant ant-hills, monkeys. Often I ate only "Salt Beef and musty biscuits."

~Things were great and "sublime" but they were also hard. I couldn't stay clean. We won't go into the details.

~When I got back to the sea near Rio de Janeiro, I was rowing myself to shore one day in order to do some collecting in a bay. A huge wave crashed over the boat. I went "head over heels," and so did all my belongings.

~You can imagine the bad words that no one heard but me. My "books, instruments & gun cases" were all floating and had to be rescued.

~I spent a whole day drying and mending things.

~Every few weeks I got some mail. Friends my age were getting married and sounded so comfortable. Sometimes I was sad I didn't have a wife — only giant fossil bones and many jars of dead creatures and plants.

~I was constantly curious and pondered all my discoveries. A lot of the time I wasn't sure what I had found.

~Sometimes I was soaring, and sometimes plodding. Often I was lonely, and lonely aches.

Who am I?

NEXT ISSUE TO COME.

FREE!

rage

PLAYER FOUR WAS in a quiet rage.

He was in the right place. He'd seen the box with his own eyes. That no-good idiot of a car thief had unloaded it at the family junk store. But how on earth would he, the rightful owner — at least the rightful thief — now figure out what had been in it?

The old man and the part-blind kid weren't acting like they'd just discovered diamonds. They didn't seem too interested in the box, aside from wanting to keep it.

What was going on?

The young kid had gone to the library that afternoon. The player followed, just to see if he could overhear anything. The boy and a friend were looking up facts about Charles Darwin. Losers — as a kid, he'd never gotten along with those bookworm types.

He needed to get back into the store and look carefully at that old bedcover. Maybe something was sewn into the lining. It'd been done before.

Old Man Chamberlain had been watching him, noticed him looking at the box, and wouldn't sell. He'd have to do it when the geezer wasn't around.

There was only one way to do that.

circling

BEFORE GOING OUR separate ways that afternoon, Lorrol and I had agreed not to tell anyone, not even family, about the *Gas Gazette*. Not yet. It would be a surprise.

But talking about Darwin: That was okay. After all, Lorrol still had to get her mom off the camp idea and convince her that her daughter had worthwhile things to investigate, work that could only be done in the library.

As soon as I walked in the door, I shot up to my room, knelt down, and pulled out the Danger Box. There were chores to do before dinner, but I needed to be sure the notebook was still there, and the *Beagle* part real.

I turned the pages, imagining it on board a ship, maybe with light coming in a porthole . . . imagining the person who wrote it . . . yes, here it was: *The Beagle called in on the 23rd of April.* I ran my finger lightly across the words, stopping on each one. There was a *reason* this notebook was a treasure, if only I could figure it out. That sticky-voiced man in the store must know something I didn't. Well, I was determined: I'd find the answer tonight. "I will," I whispered to myself. If Gas could puzzle through a bunch of hard stuff even when he felt jittery, so could I!

"How was your afternoon, Zoomy?" Gam asked at dinner. She'd made grilled hot dogs, just like Gumps said, with homemade baked beans; this usually vanished in a split second, but tonight we boys weren't eating. My grandpa was quiet. I rolled my dog from one side of the plate to the other, too excited to eat.

"Great," I said. "Lorrol and I were reading about Charles Darwin's life. He was an awesome guy."

I heard Gumps look up quickly.

"Anything to do with that old notebook?" he boomed.

"I wish," I said truthfully. "But seriously, have you ever heard people in Three Oaks talk about evolution?"

There was a moment of silence. Gam said slowly, "Hmm. Not really."

"But didn't you study Darwin in school?" I asked.

Another moment of silence. "No, now I think back. It was kind of a not-polite topic," she said.

"Why? What's rude?" I asked.

"It's kinda complicated," my grandpa said. "Especially

for some religious folks who don't believe Darwin and God belong in the same sentence. I guess it's easier not to mention his ideas. Somehow, everyone hears about what evolution means — you know, survival of the fittest and plants and animals changing over time, that stuff — but we never studied any details. Odd when you think that we're an old farming community, but there it is. We got along fine without it, and we're still doing okay." He shrugged and added, "I guess."

We were all quiet for a moment. Gam cleared her throat.

"Actually, I just read a fascinating article at the dentist's office about teaching evolution in schools. There's quite a fight going on all over the U.S. now."

"What kind of fight?" I asked.

"Well, scientists and lots of others believe evolution *must* be taught. It shouldn't be skipped over — not only because it's one of the biggest ideas ever to come along, but also because it's about how we see our world. I guess there's worry that if students can ignore evolution, they might feel free to ignore other kinds of science, which could be a dangerous thing. We need our kids to become smart scientists and keep working on a whole bunch of problems, you know?"

Gam paused and looked at Gumps, who didn't seem to be listening.

"Yup," I said. "Like Pathological Myopia, crops that can stop world hunger, how to save the environment, all that kind of stuff."

My grandma put down her fork. "Exactly. And this article said that we're one of the few big, powerful countries with a whole mess of people who believe you can't respect Darwin's scientific thinking *and* the Bible: *Can't love 'em both*, that's their message. And if it's one or the other, then suddenly we have a war between science and religion. It turns into a battle with our kids caught bang-smack in the middle. I say, why can't a person believe in both evolution and God? It's salt and pepper. Why do they have to choose? Hey, eat some of that dog, will you?"

"Wow," I said, my mouth full. "That's intense. I like the salt-and-pepper idea."

"So you can teach us more about Darwin as you learn, Zoomy!" Grandma Al said lightly as she cleared the table. "Gumps and I would love to hear."

"I think people would like him if they knew him," I said.

"I'm sure," Gam said, scraping plates.

"Back to the notebook," Gumps growled, and sighed. It was one of those extreme blasts that practically blew the silverware off the table. "This is serious. We need to tell the police we have that box, and turn over everything that was in it. Your grandma and I have decided."

"But what if that gets Buckeye in trouble for taking something he didn't know he was taking?" I asked quickly.

"Well, I've thought of that, too, but we can't go breaking the law by withholding suspicious goods. We probably should've told Officer Nab about that box when he was at the house. Whoever that man in the store was today, he didn't come to Three Oaks on vacation. He came for a reason. That's enough for me."

"Okay," I said, my mind racing. "But can I still look at the notebook tonight?"

Gumps paused for a moment, then shrugged. "Sure," he said. "It's only the difference of a few hours. I'll call the cops first thing in the morning, and I'm gonna describe that spooky fella. I've been around long enough to know when someone's up to no good."

What we didn't know was that a person was walking softly through the trees and bushes at the edge of our property. Circling the outside of the house. Watching the top of my head in front of the kitchen sink. Seeing my grandparents crisscrossing the kitchen and putting things away. Noticing the kitchen light go out an hour later. Seeing my bedroom light go on upstairs.

"Dang!" he muttered when he stepped heavily into our garden. One of the low stakes stabbed him in the knee. He pulled it out angrily and snapped it in two.

tell me

I COULDN'T WAIT to open the Danger Box that night.

In one short day, I'd found out an amazing amount. I knew that -Darwin kept lots of notebooks, -exploring nature was a big deal in those days, -Darwin had been on the *Beagle* when the notebook I was holding was written. I also knew that evolution was in the news, which might make this notebook even more valuable to someone. . . .

The Beagle called in on the 23rd of April. This afternoon, I'd asked Lorrol what she thought that meant, pretending I'd just read the "called in" while I was doing research. Lorrol didn't know the phrase, either. We decided it might mean the boat came to shore.

I went back to that page, then flipped forward and backward. Wait — I had to get organized. Digging under my bed for my P notebook — that's the one for private secrets — I opened to a fresh section. I'd write down every word I could read. I would turn myself into a sponge and try to soak up as much as I could possibly hold.

I went back to the beginning and noted the words I'd read last night and the night before. I also tried to remember the *look* of each page. I told myself that each page might hold a secret, and every word mattered. Whoa, this was slow going — if only the handwriting was neater.

Soon I was beyond the part I'd read before. There was the word *Lima*. Two lines later, *Foxes & Mice & Rats*. Down at the bottom of the page, I picked up *Chart*.

Next page, *river course* and *sand & shingle*. Later on, *Difficulty of understanding*, although I couldn't figure out the words that followed it.

Cliffs . . . above sea . . . cannot understand . . . and the single word *Islands* with a circle around it.

I turned the page. Now *white powder*, followed by some columns of numbers. Farther down, *Natural History*.

Reached Lima, Wednesday . . . Next page, I picked out *like mermaids, could not keep eyes away from them*. The pages right after were written in staggery letters, with lots crossed off. I saw the word *Islands* again.

Salt and *Sandstone* turned up a few times. And *Lima*. Later, *carriages or carts, mules & water, donkeys*.

This notebook keeper was definitely traveling in the same way Darwin had: by sea and by land. And this was a person studying nature. And mermaids!

I turned more pages, doing my best but still only deciphering an occasional word. All the scribbled-over places didn't make it easier.

Then I read *Galapagos. Ping!*

A couple of pages later, *Banana!!* Just like that, with the exclamation marks. I picked out single words and made them into a list: *sweet, sugar, supper, fish, catch, horse, cascades, steaming hot, wonderful view, valley, angular, dogs, granite, Icebergs.*

Then, *Saturday 17th Ship came*. This traveler was on and off a ship, just as Darwin had been.

My list went on: *cactus, excavate, Iguana, craters*, and a bunch of what looked like temperatures. Then, *Out of wind 108*. Unbearably hot!

And some phrases: *Eats very deliberately, without chewing . . . Iguana shakes head vertically . . . hind legs stretched out walks very slowly . . .*

Whoa, I'd read about iguanas and huge tortoises on the Galápagos today. The notebook keeper and Darwin were almost certainly in the same neighborhood. For the second time today, a giant hope bubbled up inside me. *Could it be?* Could this notebook possibly have belonged to the great Charles Darwin himself? Could I, Zoomy Chamberlain, be holding one of the most important notebooks of all time? No, it was too impossible! Plus, wouldn't Lorrol or I have read something about it today, if one of his notebooks had been stolen and never found?

Next I puzzled out *Whaler gave us water* — a whale ship! Everyone must have been wicked thirsty with those temperatures. Then *Islands* again, and *Iguana* and *eggs.* A few pages later, *Slept there Eating tortoise . . . By the way delicious in Soup.* And then, suddenly, *Galapagos Lava.*

For a moment I squeezed my eyes shut and wished, wished, wished for the notebook to let me in, for it to let me see what the writer was seeing.

I pretended to open my eyes and find I was on the Galápagos Islands, sitting on a boulder writing. A tortoise lumbered by and an iguana paused to see what I was doing.

"Tell me who I am," I whispered to the notebook.

medicin

WHEN GAM KNOCKED on my bedroom door and said, "It's very late, Zoomy. Lights out," I practically jumped out of my skin.

"Just a few more minutes," I called back.

Working as quickly as I could, I added: *pumice*, the phrase *I now understand, curious, escape, deep, circular, surface, low trees, ocean*, and the phrase *Eating a Prickly Pear*.

Or was that a *tricky* pear?

My eyes were now burning with tiredness, but I wanted to look at every page. The last few had *Eel* and *Saturday: Left our anchorage & stood out to outside of Island*.

Then a hard-to-read list: it included *Books, Barometer, Medicin, Sweet smelling oil, Black ribbon*.

I knew *medicine* had an *e* at the end. Darwin had been a bad speller. My heart did a quick thumpa-bump.

I thought of the man cruising around the store this

morning, and how worried Gumps had been. That man was looking for something that was stored inside the box. And he wanted it. Badly. Why was this notebook so valuable to him?

I looked quickly through the last few pages, taking more notes: *Islands* again, *shell-fish*, *Blue Beads*, *Fossil shells*. Another long shopping list, this one horribly scribbled out, had *Letter paper, tea, instructions, shoe, hat, candles*. And a lot more that I couldn't read. Then, *pistols*. Whoa! I knew Darwin had carried a gun.

A printed label on the inside back cover said *Velvet Paper Memorandum Book.*

I closed the notebook and ran my fingers lightly over the cover, trying to memorize the geography of every scratch, stain, and worn spot. It was red leather with a brass clasp on the edge. The metal was tarnished and speckly in one area. The lower left corner of the front label had torn off. The notebook was close to square, and about as big as my hand with fingers spread.

I wrote down these details, trying to catch and preserve everything I could see.

Until Gumps handed over this treasure to the police,

where could I hide it? The house seemed so obvious. What was an unlikely but safe spot?

Yes! Perfect. I rewrapped the notebook and tucked it back into the Danger Box. I opened my bedroom door and peered out into the dark hall.

I didn't need much light. My feet knew the way.

The Gas Gazette: Issue Eleven

~Have you ever had an experience that was not fun while it was going on but amazing to think about once it was over? That's what happened to me when we stopped at some islands in the Pacific Ocean.

~Most were jagged, black lava and "frying hot." Honestly, they looked like the "Infernal regions," if you get what I mean. A thermometer stuck in dark sand went up to 137 degrees. Rainwater collected only in small, steamy potholes in the "boisterous" swirls of volcanic rock. We were thirsty, thirsty, thirsty.

~Giant iguanas and tortoises were everywhere, and tame — I felt as though I was on "some other planet." The iguanas were three to four feet long, and the older tortoises at least two hundred pounds. I rode on the backs of several of these creatures and they hardly noticed, even when I tumbled off. The iguanas were "quick & clumsy," and I wrote in my notebook that they were "hideous," but that was probably because I was so thirsty and in such a rotten mood that I was ready to drink any form of liquid.

~We had to kill some of the giant turtles for eating, and I sipped the clear liquid in a bladder. If you don't know what body part that is, look it up.

Who am I?

NEXT ISSUE TO COME.

FREE!

by heart

HOLDING THE DANGER Box in front of me, I tip-
toed across the kitchen in my pajamas and bare feet.
Slowly, slowly I slid open the bolt to the back door. I
turned the handle.

Think like a list, I told myself. One thing at a
time. If Charles Darwin could handle a violently
pounding heart, upset stomach, and fears about dying
at sea, I could make it to the toolshed. In the dark.
Alone.

I knew the way by heart.

At night I can smell things even better than in
the daytime, especially during summer. Maybe it's
something about the heat from the sun making
the earth cook all day, like a recipe smell that
stays in a kitchen. Maybe it's also my hound-
dog nose.

As I pushed open the screen door and closed it carefully behind me, I smelled:

-gasoline from the road,

-a whiff of burned meat from our grill, and

-lavender blossoms.

I knew exactly how many steps it was to the toolshed. I started walking.

Have you ever noticed that wind comes alive in the dark? It suddenly feels as though it means what it does, like the leaves are shushing for a reason and the sheet waving gently on the clothesline is saying something.

Over heeere! No, heeere! Lost, lost, lost! the wind seemed to be whispering.

I kept moving, and felt braver every time I thought about Darwin struggling with his fears. *I can do this*, I told the wind.

The grass was cool and wet. *Eight, nine, ten* . . . Now I was past the clothesline. I looked straight ahead and saw only blackness. I spun around and checked for the blur of what I thought was the porch light behind me. *Bad idea*, I told myself fiercely. *Don't look back.*

At step thirteen I smelled the tomatoes in the garden. Red. Sweet. *Fourteen, fifteen, sixteen* . . .

Now I smelled only trees. I wondered for a moment

if I had headed in the wrong direction. *Black equals wind equals Deeps*, I thought to myself. *No need to be afraid.*

Hugging the Danger Box, I held my left hand in front of me so I wouldn't bump into anything.

My heart was beating like crazy, and suddenly I remembered Harold and his purple crayon. Harold out there with the dragon. Harold and my new friend Gas. They'd both done much harder things; I could do this.

Nineteen, twenty . . . My hand touched wood.

I felt along the side of the shed until I got to the door. I opened it and slipped inside.

bang!

I KNEW JUST where everything was. I slid the Danger Box into a gap between an old bag of cement and a stack of paint cans. There — safe and hidden. No one would ever guess this box held a treasure.

I opened the box once more to check on the notebook. *I'll be back*, I promised. *Sorry you're buried out here.*

186

Just then a car sped by on our road, and light tipped into the high window of the shed. It was at that moment, the Danger Box open, that I heard the footsteps. They were soft but heavy.

Thump-squish, thump-scree, thump-squish.

Someone walking, and it wasn't one of my grandparents. *Uh-oh-oh-oh-uh-oh. Close the door.*

I knew it wouldn't squeak if I pulled it slowly. Somehow, I did.

The steps stopped outside the shed. I was afraid of making even the tiniest sound.

Thump, whump, thump! I was sure whoever was outside could hear my heart.

And then, out in the Deeps, the night exploded.

BANG!

running

IT WAS THE loudest firecracker I'd ever heard.

The steps outside the shed began to run. I listened to them running until the wind took them away. I closed the top of the Danger Box, my fingers strange and shaky. More light poured in the toolshed window.

I pushed open the shed door, thinking I saw our kitchen light. I didn't. It was a huge paleness, behind the entire house. In town. For a moment I thought I'd fallen asleep in the shed, dreamed the footsteps, and that this was dawn.

Then I smelled fire.

The siren on Elm Street began whoop-whooping.

Our kitchen door bounced open and I heard Gam calling, "Zoomy! *Zoomy!* Oh, thank the Lord. What on earth are you doing out here?"

As I hurried toward the house, Gumps shouted, "Goin' downtown!"

Gam said, "I'm not letting you go near a fire without me, Ash." She had on her flowered bathrobe, the one with a hole in the elbow. "Hurry up, Zoomy!" She grabbed me, gave a quick hug, and pushed me into the entryway.

"Get your sneakers! We're going, too." I saw that my grandpa's pajamas were poking out the bottom of his pants. I grabbed his gardening shirt off a hook and put it on over my pajamas.

We could see blue police lights through the trees. People were shouting. The hubbub was coming from the area near the store.

Gumps was gone into the night, clankety-clank running, before we got down the steps. Gam grabbed my hand, something she hadn't done for ages, and we hurried as fast as we could go. She gave me huff-puff warnings about curbs and dips. We crossed the train tracks.

Then I heard my grandma say, "Oh, dear God. No, please, no!"

burning

IT WAS THE store.

-Flames
-Smoke
-Burning
-Burning
-Burning

Our lives were burning.

Emergency lights. Running footsteps. I heard my grandma shout, "Ash! No! No! Don't you go in there!"

Then she let go of my hand, and I stood still. I knew she had to disappear. It hurt to breathe. Everyone was coughing. Someone in a black, slippery coat spun me around. "Only firemen in this area!" he bellowed.

I took three steps. Tripped. Fell. Got up.

And then a tremendous, shattering *CRACK*. Glass exploding.

Even I could see it: a Deep of fire. Flames with a brightness as big as trees.

My body was whumpa-whumping so wildly it didn't feel like mine. I imagined all those treasures being burned alive: my red sofa, the mouse in the sugar bowl, the crocodile. My science encyclopedia. The horseshoes. In a moment I'd explode, too; I'd shoot into the cool Deep of sky. I'd wake up and find it was only a nightmare.

The crowd was swelling. More voices. "Here, son," the janitor from school said, and taking me by the shoulders, he helped me away from the heat. "Aren't you the Chamberlain kid? Sit right here on this curb."

He disappeared, too. I sat.

A moment later, a hospital stretcher bumped past me. Someone was moaning. I saw blood on the side of a man's head. Then I recognized the fishing-worm eyebrow and a clump of matted hair: It was Buckeye.

What was *he* doing out here? I had to tell my grandparents! *I should have told sooner, before this happened. Why did I listen to him?*

The moaning went on, and I realized it was me. I tried to get up, but my legs had lost their bones. I put my head down on my knees. *Please, please* was as far as I could get. *Please.*

Then someone was patting my back. "Zoomy," a shaky voice said. "I'm so, so sorry. Mom, this is my friend Zoomy! And that was their family store. Hey, where's your grandma and grandpa?"

I was stuck. I put my head up, but no words came out.

"Lorrol, you stay here," a woman said. "I'll find them, and also see if anyone needs my help."

Lorrol and I sat side by side. She was quiet. I don't know if I was. Then, as if she understood I wanted company but not too much, she moved closer so that our shoulders were touching. Then her shoulder went up and down, and I realized she was crying.

watching a death

SOON LORROL WAS gone and my grandparents were down on the ground next to me. We three were hugging as close as:

-Burrs
-Melted Cough Drops in a Hot Pocket

"Was that Buckeye?" I asked the wrinkles in my grandpa's neck. His whiskery skin nodded.

Gam spoke first. "Yes. Taken to the hospital. They said he'll recover." Her voice wobbled like I'd never heard it before, and Gumps stayed quiet. Dead silent but jittery-splat — I knew because his throat was pumping up and down and swallowing lots, like mine when I'm upset.

"I saw him," I said.

Gam sniffed hard and wiped her nose on her sleeve, something she'd taught me not to do. Then she turned her cheek my way, and I followed a jagged streak of soot from her forehead to her chin. Her face looked broken, like a cracked egg.

I put my hand out to touch the line.

Hugging and weeping in the middle of Elm Street: For us, this was a shocker. When we looked up, we saw fire trucks everywhere. My grandparents told me that help from the next town had arrived. I had never seen so much squinty light.

I remember:

-rolling deeps of yellow and white and blue
-roaring, popping, crackling, creaking
-heavy things falling
-china and glass smashing
-the whoosh and sob of red-hot wind

I'd never known a building could be in pain. It was -like we were watching a death. -Like that dying hurt. -Like a part of our family was -burning, -burning, -burning.

Our hearts were on fire.

blame

THE OWNERS OF the sandwich shop, Bob and Dorothy, got us home. They helped us three into the cab of a truck, and my head knocked against a fishing pole as we drove. In our kitchen, we found an uncut pie and a huge pitcher of ice-cool lemonade; that's the kindness of neighbors. In the scramble to get out, we hadn't locked the door.

I thought of the notebook and was glad it was safe. Hidden.

But I felt terrible about having kept the Buckeye secret. So I told, right then and there, at the kitchen table. It was a relief to unload the story about the library visit and the threats. Maybe Buckeye had been so angry at us that he'd burned the store down.

"Oh, Zoomy!" Gam said. "This definitely wasn't your fault. I can't imagine what Buckeye was trying to get you to do, anyway. He was probably out of his mind. Crazy with alcohol."

Gumps shook his head. "This was my fault. I

should've offered to help him that night at the house instead of pushing him away. Instead of treating him like a healthy man. God forgive me."

Now my grandpa buried his head in his hands. Gam and I both patted his arm. He didn't seem to feel it.

A long groan came from deep in his throat. "I was nearby when the firemen found him inside the back door. Buckeye was muttering. I leaned close to him and said, 'Son.' He said, 'Tried. I tried to stop it.'"

"Ohhh!" My grandma and I both made the same sound.

"Poor thing," she said. "Maybe he did."

My grandpa groaned again. "Problem is, the box and the blanket are now gone, either burned or taken, and we'll never know which. I'll bet that man who was in the store came back. Took them. Searched for the missing notebook, didn't find it, and then set a fire, either in anger or just to cover his tracks. And Buckeye — who knows what he was doing, but it doesn't look good."

"I have the notebook," I said. "It's safe."

"Which means we're not," Gumps growled. "Nor is Buckeye. What if that same creep thinks one of us in the family has it? Better go get the thing, and we'll hand it over to the police. Now."

"Okay." I got up, my heart suddenly feeling like it weighed a thousand pounds. "So if I hadn't kept it, maybe this wouldn't have happened. Buckeye and the store wouldn't be burned." I began tapping my chin. Tapping and tapping.

A voice inside my head was saying, *My* - tap! - *fault* - tap! - *My* - tap! - *fault* - tap!

"Stop that now!" Gumps burst out. "Every step in life makes something else happen, and we all do the best we can. Right? Right! No more of this blame talk. We're done with that."

"Hodilly-hum," Gam added.

I nodded, and did feel better. The tapping stopped.

Outside the kitchen door, I looked back toward town. I could still hear the fire engines thrumming, and I knew the destruction and hurt were not over. I sent a silent message toward the part of our family that was once the store, and all the things I'd loved and grown up with: *We won't forget you. Ever, ever, ever.*

I put one foot in front of the other.

The Gas Gazette: Issue Twelve

A FREE NEWSPAPER ABOUT A MYSTERIOUS SOUL

~Exploring these ten sizzling islands was like scrambling around on the top of a stove — I don't think I was at my best. I collected lots of little birds and samples of the huge reptiles, but my sorting and labeling was parboiled in the heat, and I wasn't as careful as I was in some other places.

~My metal pencil became so hot it was hard to grip. Sweat dripped on my notebook.

~Criminals, pirates, and a sad sailor or two had been abandoned on these islands. We found a human skull.

~I was happy to leave. But I never forgot those few scalding days. I saw small differences between the same kinds of creatures, island to island. How and why? This curious subject got me thinking.

~I have gone over every detail of those few amazing days in my mind, and often wished I could have a do-over on some of my warmer moments.

~It's tough to do excellent work in extreme heat.

~I did keep one baby tortoise as a pet. I never dreamed he would live far longer than any of us on board that ship.

Who am I?

NEXT ISSUE TO COME.

FREE!

the weight of the night

OPENING THE SHED door, I stepped right into the Danger Box. *Crunch!* went the firecracker shells under my sneaker.

I knew before I knew. The next few moments on my hands and knees were endless. I felt around the bottom of the box, fingers spread as if they could catch what was already missing.

As if the box weren't -out of its hiding place and -open.

Then the weight of the night fell down on me. It was the fire, strangling guilt about Buckeye, the death of the store, the notebook: I couldn't breathe. Suddenly I was lying on the floor of the toolshed, feeling the cool cement under my cheek.

The Danger Box, just beyond my nose, had splinters on it. Blue paint. A tiny piece of label with a red cherry on it. Then the side of the box was spinning away down a tunnel, farther and farther away, and I was gone.

one piece

GUMPS SAID HE almost collapsed when he went out to the shed and found me passed out on the floor. He carried me into the kitchen, and that's when Gam fell apart. "I haven't seen her sob like that since the day you turned up on the kitchen steps in the cat carrier, way back when," my grandpa told me later. "Who woulda believed your world could explode so many times in one day?"

I woke up with an ice bag on my head. We were all three on the sofa, and I was in the middle. I guess it was good right then just to be alive and together. We didn't have much to say.

Then the local *and* state police came by, Gam put on her apron, made several pots of strong coffee, and cut the pie. The police told her and Gumps the news. I listened from the sofa. It wasn't pretty.

-Buckeye had been living in an old storage room on the second floor of the Three Oaks Pharmacy for some time, helping himself to food and liquor from the grocery section at night. A bed made of old towels was surrounded by a mess of empty beer bottles and beef jerky wrappers.

-He was in trouble for breaking and entering, trespassing, a bunch of thefts, and maybe arson. After all, he'd been found inside the back door to our store, someone had clearly punched in the glass above the lock, and the police had no other suspects. A search within a five-mile radius of Three Oaks turned up the stolen Ford truck. It was inside a deserted barn just down the road.

-The police hadn't questioned Buckeye yet, but would as soon as the hospital allowed it. He was being treated for burns on his neck and arms, cuts and scrapes, smoke inhalation, and alcohol poisoning.

-Gumps told the police about his son's unhappy visit several weeks earlier, about the box he left in the garage, saying it was "for the store," and about how we finally unpacked it and found only an old blanket and a scribbled-up notebook.

-He also explained that I was a notebook keeper, and they'd allowed me to look at it for a couple of days before turning it over to the police, not thinking it was a big deal. Then an unfriendly visitor walked into the store yesterday morning and was clearly angry that my grandpa wouldn't sell him the box and blanket. Late that night, I'd hidden the notebook in the toolshed for safekeeping but someone had taken it during the fire.

-My grandpa did his best to describe the man in the store.

-The police wanted to ask me some questions but said it could wait until tomorrow.

Then the screen door banged shut as the officers left. It was quiet in the kitchen while my grandparents cleaned up. I lay on the sofa and thought. Or tried to — my head felt like it was jammed with thoughts that were all bumping into each other.

Gam called in from the next room, "Your friend Lorrol and her mom are good people."

"Yup," I said, and suddenly my stomach churned with sadness. The *Gas Gazette* seemed far away, and Darwin even farther.

Would Lorrol be angry when she heard I'd had a special, old notebook, something that mentioned the *Beagle,* and had kept it a secret when we were research-ing Darwin yesterday? Would she understand why I couldn't tell?

Would my grandparents? If I told now that I thought

the notebook really *was* valuable, I might make things worse for Buckeye. What if it was worth even more than the stolen truck?

This was not a comfortable secret, but I couldn't let it out. Not now. I realized I might never find out what I'd been holding last night, or who wrote it. Not without hurting someone else.

I remembered how Lorrol had described Darwin's tree of life as an odd jigsaw puzzle. Suddenly that felt comforting. I thought: *Maybe everyone's life is a big, hoped-for plan with missing pieces, pieces that you only glimpse now and then. Kind of like the way my eyes work; you only get to see what's right around you. And you never stop hoping or praying that you'll run across what fits.*

Like Gumps hoping he could keep the store open. Like me hoping I could make a great discovery that would add the piece he needed. Like Gam hoping that Buckeye really *had* tried to stop that fire.

The notebook had been a piece of my life, it *belonged* in our family puzzle, and someone had stolen it.

It was in my hands, I found myself thinking, *-in -my -hands.*

The Gas Gazette: Issue Thirteen

A FREE NEWSPAPER ABOUT A MYSTERIOUS SOUL

~I have seen some terrible things in my life, and been unable to stop them.

~In South America I saw "heart-sickening" treatment of slaves. One child, perhaps six or seven, handed me a not-perfectly-clean glass of water and was beaten with a horsewhip. I have heard the screams of household slaves who were tortured without mercy after making the smallest mistake. How can anyone do this to another human being? Slavery is an "odious, deadly" evil.

~I've had to witness the pain of those I loved dearly, and been unable to help. The illness of one's child is perhaps the worst.

~Two of our babies died when young, a boy and a girl, and one daughter at age ten. When she died, I didn't think I could live. My heart was broken, and hurt beyond what words can say.

~I have spent most of my life battling stomach problems that made me feel wretched and weak;

cures have helped but do not last. Without the care of my loving wife I don't think I could have lived as long.

~Survival is sometimes a mixed blessing.

Have you ever felt this way?

Who am I?

NEXT ISSUE TO COME.

FREE!

a pebble in the pie

I SLEPT LATE the next morning, and was halfway through a bowl of cold cereal when there was a knock at the kitchen door. My grandma went to answer it, and I quickly twisted my pajamas around so the fly wasn't right in front. I tried to straighten my glasses, which Gam had mended with masking tape. One stem had snapped when I'd fizzed out on the toolshed floor.

"Hello," I said.

"Hello, son," Officer Nab said. "We've met before. Mind if we talk?"

I shook my head.

"We know about the box with the blanket and notebook, the one transported by your — ah, father. Your grandparents said you spent some time looking at that notebook. Can you describe it for me?"

I nodded. "It was hard to read because the handwriting wasn't neat and most of it was crossed out. But I took notes."

"I see," the officer said, pulling out a pad. He paused, pencil over the blank page.

"I'll get them," I offered. As I headed upstairs, I heard my grandma telling the officer about my eyesight. She also said I was a good boy.

Why was it that keeping a secret felt wrong? Maybe secrets were natural — after all, I was a Secret from a Secret from a Secret, and my grandparents had always told me that was a good thing. A *blessing* . . . maybe this secret was a blessing, too. A crossed-out one. Crossed out but not gone.

I sat down cheerfully and opened the notebook I'd been writing in the night before. "These are some of the words I figured out," I began. "They include: -sand, -sea, -rats, -dogs, -sugar, -catch. . . ." I carefully left out Galapagos, Islands, iguanas, and tortoises. I turned the page. "Oh, and -boat, -fish, -supper, -wind, -water, -eggs, -walks . . ."

I pretended I didn't notice Officer Nab sighing in a bored way.

"I was very excited because I found the date 1835 inside the front, and not many old, scribbled-on note-books survive that long, you know?" I said, as if he should know. "But no name," I added mournfully. "No tellin' whose it was, especially now."

I heard another puff of air, this one louder, and the swish of fabric as he uncrossed his legs in his uniform. "Well, thank you, son," he began. "Don't think there's any need . . ."

I was looking at my notes again. "Oh, how about -soup, -cliffs, -horse, -biscuits, -river . . . ?"

The officer cleared his throat. "Very helpful. We'll be back in touch if we need more detail. We know where to come."

I nodded, and tried to look slightly disappointed. Gam ruffled my hair.

He stood, hesitated for a moment, and said, "You were in your grandpa's store when a man came in and wanted to buy that box and the blanket."

"Yes," I said.

"Were you — ah, able to see this man?"

I shook my head. "But I heard what he said. He wasn't too nice-sounding once he found out the box wasn't for sale."

"Yes, that's what your grandpa told me, too," the officer said. "And that you hid the notebook in your toolshed because you thought that was an extra-safe place. Well, this is a start," he said, closing the notebook.

"Bye now," I said. "Thanks for visiting," I added, trying to sound as if I spent all day waiting for visitors.

After she showed the policeman out, Gam said, "So . . . where's the pebble in the pie, young man?"

I grinned. This was what my grandma always said when she knew I was hiding something.

"Not exactly a pebble," I said. "Maybe more of a huge berry."

"I see." She smiled, and swatted me with her dish towel. "Cough it up."

"I left off a few words back there, like *Galapagos* and *Islands*, because I didn't want the police to know how valuable the notebook might be. Because as long as they're suspecting Buckeye, that's not fair. To him. I mean, he probably didn't know what he'd taken. . . ."

"I see," my grandma said again. "Go on."

I sighed. "I'm pretty disappointed," I said. This was one hundred percent now, no sugar added. "I think the notebook was kept by someone who might have known Charles Darwin, because his ship the *Beagle* was mentioned. For a while I even thought it was Darwin *himself*!

I know that sounds nuts, but the person who kept this notebook went to some of the same places in the same year, and there are details that fit, like his lists and his bad spelling. Lorrol and I were just starting to research Darwin's life yesterday. . . ."

"Oh, yes," my grandma said slowly. "You told us how excited you were. Does Lorrol know about the notebook?"

"No."

"You haven't told her about it?"

I shook my head. "This may not sound too good, but I was thinking of something sneaky that would help our family. Gumps told me yesterday that the store was in trouble, and we might have to close. I thought maybe, if the notebook was valuable, we could sell it and get money that would help us save the store, even though the notebook might not exactly have been ours. Buckeye *did* give it to you guys, right?"

Gam's voice wasn't mad when she said, "The old, 'Don't ask, can't tell'?"

"Yup, I guess so. But I knew we planned to give the notebook to the police this morning, and I wanted to know as much as I could, just in case — well, in case it helped us survive. That's why I stayed up late and took notes. So we'd have a record of what we had. And that's why I hid it in the toolshed, just to confuse anyone bad who might be looking."

"I'd call it a berry," Gam said. "And we'll tell the police when we cut into that pie, if we do. How's that?"

"Deal," I said. "So Lorrol and I can keep researching?"

"Don't see why not. But if she's really a friend . . . hmm, people don't like to be kept in the dark too long, you know?"

"I know. I'll tell her, and explain about how I hoped the notebook might fit into saving our family. It was kind of a dream."

"Speaking of saving, your grandpa went downtown ages ago. Said he had to speak to the insurance people. At least there's the blessing of fire insurance to balance out all the losses. Where could he be?"

The word *be* was just coming out of her mouth when we heard my grandpa clumping up the kitchen steps, sounding as though each foot weighed a million pounds. My grandma hurried to open the door.

"Oh, Ash!" she said. "What is it, dear?"

I knew this was serious; my grandma only said *dear* to my grandpa when something very bad had happened.

fried squirrel

GUMPS CIRCLED THE kitchen table twice before he said anything. Every once in a while he moaned.

Gam and I stayed quiet. Sometimes that's the right thing to do.

Finally he pulled out his chair, sat down, and blurted, "No insurance. I dropped it a coupla years ago, after paying all my dang-blast life. Just trying to save us a little money. Thought I might be able to get some of it back, but that's not the game. It's gone, every last nickel."

My ears were a little shocked, but my heart wasn't. Gam only said, "Ohhhh," like a balloon that was losing air.

My grandpa seemed to have gotten about a dozen more wrinkles in his hands, just overnight. My grandma reached over and put her hands on his. Then I put my hands on the pile, in between theirs: Four wrinkly pinks with blue veins, and two light browns.

"We will be okay," Gam said. "Even if we have to eat squirrel."

"Or Hand Sandwich," I added, trying to be funny.

Gumps snorted, and I don't know if it was a laugh or a sob or both. "Tastes like chicken," he said.

Things were getting stranger by the minute.

"We'll try it fried," Gam said, in her best hodilly-hum tone. Her voice was shaky but determined not to be.

Were they *serious*?

It's a strange thing, how people are sometimes supposed to hide things and sometimes not. Especially around the people they love.

I thought squirrel sounded disgusting, but I kept that a secret.

The Gas Gazette: Issue Fourteen

~When I returned from the trip, I was thrilled to see my family, plumbing, and English food.

~As a university student years before, my friends and I had started a "Glutton Club" and tried to shock ourselves by dining on "strange flesh," like owls and other creatures not usually eaten. We thought that was adventuresome, but little did I know . . .

~While traveling, I ate many insects, some by mistake, and lots of creatures I'd never dreamed of putting in my mouth. In addition to odd fish, shellfish, and reptiles, we lived on ostrich, armadillo, deer, agouti (a large rodent), even puma.

~We purchased some difficult-to-identify meats while stopping for supplies: Don't ask, not sure.

~It was a good rule on our voyage not to think while eating.

~Lots of insects ate *us*.

~Sometimes I believe that being bitten by an insect I called "Benchuca," a nasty South American parasite, made me ill for the rest of my life.

~But then how do you explain how dreadfully sick I got before leaving England, long before any strange bug bites? My stomach has always worried.

~Discovery makes me feel better.

~What would life be without wonder?

Who am I?

NEXT ISSUE TO COME.

FREE!

lemon in the wound

AFTER THE NO Insurance news, in those hours after the fire, it seemed like my grandparents couldn't see real well, either.

The kitchen got too quiet, even before dinner. Gumps went out to pick some green beans, and stepped on a bunch of zucchini blossoms while he was picking. I offered to help him, but he only shrugged.

Next we heard a shriek from the kitchen. Gam had been slicing tomatoes to go with a leftover hamburger casserole, and moved on to her finger. She had to squeeze it in a dish towel for a good half hour before the bleeding stopped.

Every few hours they called the hospital to check up on Buckeye, whose condition, the doctors said, was stable.

The fire had wounded us all, that's for sure. But knowing there was no insurance was like squeezing lemon in a raw cut. It hurt in a different way. My grandma had no good sayings to share, not this time.

After dinner, my grandpa offered to pick up some milk. He backed our truck out of the driveway and ran bang-smack into a huge tree trunk and knocked off the fender. He'd driven by it a thousand times.

When he returned with a half gallon, he handed it to me and I dropped it on the kitchen floor. It didn't open, but slid under the table, and I bumped my head picking it up.

"Enough accidents. Time for bed," Gam said, even though it was barely dark. We all climbed the stairs, and the house settled into a long, quiet night.

Lying in bed, I felt especially bad for Gumps. I knew he loved the store, and he'd loved it all his life. Me, too, but his life was much longer than mine.

The No Insurance was a dangerous secret, a secret that he hadn't told even my grandma, not wanting to worry her. He'd kept it for years.

What a huge hurt.

And then there was Buckeye. Buckeye was kin, that was for sure, and he was in trouble with the law. The police suspected him of setting the fire, but even I didn't think that he'd do something like that. He might have been nasty and mean, but why would he destroy our family business? It didn't make sense.

The only other possibility was the Stranger. Someone had to find him.

What if he was still in Three Oaks, trying to look innocent?

I sat straight up in bed. No one would think a mostly blind kid and a noisy girl could find a criminal, especially in a small town.

The leaves outside whispered, *loook, yessss, loook*. It seemed obvious now. Of course the man was still here. And if the man was still here, so was the notebook.

i go

THE NEXT DAY was blue times two and windless. The lack of breeze felt strange after so many weeks. In summer when the wind blows, the corn rustles in waves, acre after acre as far as the ear can hear. Our town becomes an island in a sea of swishing stalks and leaves. That morning we heard only birds and bugs: mourning doves, red-winged blackbirds, sparrows, crickets, bees. It seemed like the world was saying, *Look, I can be gentle again. And kind.*

There was no store for my grandpa to go to, so after breakfast he stomped out to our garden and started hoeing the sod at one end. "Makin' it bigger" was all he said.

"Need help?" I asked.

"Naw, your grandma said you might want to go to the library. Go on, get a break from all this — this —"

"I don't need a break," I said, not wanting to hurt my grandpa more. "But I have some research I want to do."

"Right," Gumps said, and kept working. I noticed he

slammed that hoe down into the dirt like there was no tomorrow.

Inside, Gam was baking blueberry pies. By seven that morning, she'd already pulled two out of the oven. "Button jar" was all she said. Then, looking at me, "Go to it. I'll walk you over."

I nodded, knowing she wouldn't have said that if she knew what kind of research I had in mind.

bait

I DIDN'T EXPECT all the soothing words we heard on the way to the library. We'd never had a family disaster, not that I could remember, and kept so much to ourselves that we weren't used to much back-and-forth. But our town is famous for being kind when lightning strikes, and when it hit us, kindness was everywhere.

By the time I got to the library doors, I knew that someone was bringing over a coconut cake later on; that someone else was going to use his tractor to help my grandpa start cleaning up the wreckage; that the grocery store owner was handing over an envelope filled with coupons.

And Lorrol: Her smile was shining, just like her name. I felt as though we'd been friends forever, and I didn't have to be shy about all the tears and hugs the night before last.

"I have important stuff to tell you," I said right away. "Let's go behind the library and talk."

"Okay," she said, but didn't ask any questions. Lorrol

always seemed to know when to be ready for something Big. We waded through waist-high weeds and wildflowers, and sat side by side on the hood of an abandoned car.

"I wrote three issues of the *Gas Gazette* yesterday!" she said. "I was so sad, I just got to work."

I nodded. "Good idea. I can't wait to read them, and to find out more about Darwin, lots more. But first I've gotta tell you a secret."

In the next half hour, I spilled the sugar on the mysterious notebook. Lorrol was quiet at first, then she grabbed a handful of Queen Anne's lace and pulled it up by the roots. I was glad I wasn't a nearby plant.

"Why didn't you tell me right away?" she blurted, but simmered down again once she'd heard more. Eventually she understood that I couldn't have told without putting a member of my family in danger.

"So how the heck can we find this stranger when you don't know what he looks like?" she asked.

"Easy. I'd recognize his voice," I said. "He makes a *wa-wa* sound, like someone eating a hot marshmallow."

"Hmmm."

"Three Oaks is so small. If he's here, he's probably right nearby, trying to look innocent. I mean, if we were visitors and just ran off after the fire, it would look suspicious, right? Also, maybe he doesn't know the notebook was the valuable thing in the box — I mean, that box was all sealed up when we got it. It's possible the stranger still thinks we're hiding something, but doesn't know what it is even though he now has the notebook. I mean, he's *gotta* be the one who took it from the toolshed, but maybe he doesn't know why I was hiding it. And maybe he's still watching us. Why don't we walk around, and — hey! We'll use me as bait!"

"Huh?" Lorrol leaned closer and looked right at me.

"He'll know who I am. And he'll know I had the notebook, because he must've seen me hide it in the shed. All you have to do is notice *who* is noticing *me*!"

"I told you Brain Boy was a good name for you!" Lorrol crowed, rocking back and forth. Suddenly she stopped.

"What?"

"How could he have been outside the toolshed when the fire was first exploding if he set it?" she asked. "You couldn't have heard Buckeye, we know that, because he was behind the store by then . . . or in it. . . ."

We were both quiet for a minute.

"Maybe the Stranger started the fire by mistake," I said. "My grandpa never allowed anyone to smoke inside the store. He used to say that it was 'dry as a plow horse at noon.' Just about all whatnots can burn or melt: books, furniture, treasures. . . . All you'd have to do is drop a cigarette or a match in there, and after a few minutes everything would explode in flames —" I broke off, remembering Lorrol's horseshoe on the red sofa. I wanted to tell her about it, but didn't dare. Suddenly my eyes were swimming.

"Zoomy? You okay to do this?"

"Just got some dirt in my eye," I said.

"So much family *soo-ris*. That's the word my mom uses when troubles are piling high on all sides."

I nodded. "That's another language?"

"Yiddish. It's spelled *t-s-u-r-i-s*."

"It sounds like a short version of Worry Crumbs Times a Million, which is definitely what we've got."

"Yup." Lorrol nodded, but then somehow knew that action would help more than sympathy. For a Firecracker, she's wise. Folding her hands under her chin, she said, "So, let's start. There's only one place in town that the Stranger could be staying: Mrs. Gander's. We could get her to talk if she's not suspicious and if he's not home."

"Right. Let's stroll toward her place, and you watch like a hawk," I said, standing up.

"Right." Lorrol nodded. "He'll be trying to look casual. Like he's not in any hurry."

"Right," I said again. Lorrol and I definitely belonged to the Same Word Club, in addition to the other ones. "I'll bet the cops have already talked with him. Any visitor stands out around here. But if Buckeye's their suspect and the Stranger is slippery, I'll bet he has an alibi and is planning to swim on out of town once he knows for sure there isn't any more treasure to be found."

"Well, we'll just have to catch him before he leaves, won't we?" Lorrol said, and I suddenly believed it. I squeezed the stem of my glasses, making sure the masking tape was on tight.

"Ready?" I asked. "You'll have to tell me whenever we get to a curb."

"Will do."

"Put me on the hook."

jam

PLAYER FOUR ORDERED *eggs over easy, hash browns, and raisin toast. He pretended to read the paper.*

The conversation swirled in currents around him:

". . . so sad . . ."

"Can't imagine the town without it . . ."

"I've heard Ash dropped his insurance . . ."

"I bought our oak dining table from his father . . ."

In a town this size, the stranger knew he had to stick around. Give it another day. He'd already explained to the cops how he'd found Three Oaks, and why — after all, the delivery job he'd been doing for Mr. Zip hadn't been illegal. He'd then identified his stolen truck, which was still in police custody, agreed to be fingerprinted, and told the police that he'd been in bed early the night of the fire and hadn't left his room.

He put down the paper in order to smear a thick spoonful of blueberry jam on his toast. Looking through the front window of the coffee shop, he caught the eye of that short girl with frizzy, black hair, the one in the library. She was walking next to the grandson with Coke-bottle glasses.

She looked right back and, turning toward the boy as they moved on, whispered something in his ear. As she glanced over her shoulder, the man gave her a little smile.

He sighed and wiped the stickiness off his fingers.

The whole situation was unfortunate. He wished he hadn't had to play a part.

a hole in the screen

"TELL MRS. GANDER you're selling something," Lorrol whispered.

I cleared my throat. "Morning," I said.

The old lady's head popped up from the hollyhocks lining her garden fence. "Oh, Zoomy!" she said, and rushed to give me a hug. "How are all of you doing?" she asked. "So terrible."

I did my best to look uncomfortable. "Could I come in for a minute to use your bathroom? Any guests at the moment?" I asked. "This is my friend Lorrol. We're just walking around and reminding folks to buy my grandma's pies. She baked a bunch this morning."

"Of course, dear! Of course," Mrs. Gander said, and hurried us both inside. We noticed the front door was standing open when we came, and she didn't close it now.

I started up the stairs as if I knew where I was going. Lorrol followed me. "Oh, ah, there is one guest staying here, but you can use the downstairs powder room," Mrs. Gander said. "Maybe that's better. . . ."

"That's okay, she'll wait outside and help me find my way down," I called back, hurrying ahead. Feeling wall tile under my hand, I ducked into a hallway bathroom and closed the door loudly.

Lorrol can be amazingly brave. As she told me later, she peeked into each of the three bedrooms. Only one had an unmade bed. And, whoa, a duffel bag with clothes. She reached into the bag and felt around. Nothing.

A screened porch outside the room! No sound from downstairs. She stepped out onto the porch and pushed on each one of the screens. Whoa! One gave. There was room for a person to squeeze out onto the roof, climb into the pine tree, and then jump to the ground — or the other way around.

Just then she heard a man's voice downstairs. It was odd and yes, kind of gooey. Nothing for it but to hurry back to the stairs and plop down. She said her heart was going double-time, and she was sure she looked as guilty as a beet.

thinking like a fish

PLONK. PLONK. PLONK. Silence. The heavy boots stopped in front of her knees. Lorrol looked up, and the stranger scowled down.

"I'm just waiting for my friend," she trumpeted in a voice that would've worked for the legally deaf. "He's legally blind. Had to use the facilities."

I got the message, and flushed the toilet twice.

"Of course," a familiar voice snarled. *Plonk, plonk, BANG:* A door slammed shut.

When I stepped out of the bathroom, Lorrol practically broke my neck. She grabbed me by the arm — "Hurry, he's in his room!" — and dragged me down the stairs so fast that I tripped and skinned my knee.

"I heard!" I whispered as we thumped along at top speed. "Slow down, will you? I don't know these stairs!"

"Something I've gotta tell you!" Lorrol whispered back.

Mrs. Gander heard all the bumping, and rushed out of the kitchen.

"Oh, my!" she said. "Still in such a hurry?"

After she'd put disinfectant on my knee and insisted we have some lemonade in the kitchen, we headed back toward town. We never did get a name.

"Sorry about that," Lorrol said. "Guess I'm a little excitable under pressure."

"Just remember that when you jerk a fishing line at the wrong time, you scare the fish," I said.

Lorrol filled me in on everything. And she said this was the same guy who'd noticed us from inside the coffee shop. Should we tell the police?

"Let's first collect a few more facts," she suggested. "Some stuff that might add up to a clue."

"Hey!" I stopped dead in my tracks. "I know what *I* would have done if I was a grown-up trying to hide that notebook."

"You mean a fishy grown-up," Lorrol added.

"Right. If I were the Fish, I wouldn't keep the notebook nearby. I'd get rid of it!"

knee-deep in whoppers

MY CHIN BARELY came up to the counter.

"Well, hello, Zoomy," the postmaster said in a pleasant voice. "So very sorry about the fire. What a loss for us all." Mr. Dither's fingers always flew around like they had their own plan. Right now they were playing with a pen attached to a chain.

"Thank you," I said. Lorrol, standing next to me, started in on the wiggling. "Could my friend use your bathroom, please?"

He sounded surprised. "Well, why, sure. Come around the counter here, and down the hall to the right, young lady. There's no one back there."

I stayed in front. It's a small space, and I knew I was the only customer.

"How's business these days?" I asked. "Lots of summer mail?"

The postmaster's voice clouded over. "Not like a few years ago, lot fewer people," he said. "But we're lucky to still have our own post office here. I count my blessings, don't get me wrong."

"I think my grandpa told a customer where to mail a small package day before yesterday, the day of the fire. I was just curious; that would've been the last sale we ever made, and I kinda think my grandpa would be happy to buy it back. You know, if the mail didn't go out and the customer agreed to sell it back."

"Know the man's name?" Mr. Dither asked.

"Just a visitor," I said. "Cash." I was now knee-deep in whoppers.

"Too bad. Several people did mail packages yesterday morning, but the post went out in the afternoon, I'm afraid."

"Was one a fi — I mean, a stranger with a kind of sticky voice?" I asked. "If not, I can probably find him in town — that is, if he's still around," I blundered on. "I'd recognize his speech."

"You're a regular detective," the postmaster said. A thick rubber band was now riding around on his first two fingers. "Sorry I can't be more helpful, Zoomy. You're one thoughtful grandson."

Lorrol was back, and tapping me impatiently on the shoulder like she had something to tell.

"See you, thanks!" I said, turning to go.

"You'll never guess what!" Lorrol whispered as she pulled open the door.

The stamp box clattered off the counter behind us. I knew the sound; I'd seen it happen before. As the door jingled shut, I pictured Mr. Dither's fingers cleaning up and being glad they had something to do.

hot, then cool

"MR. DITHER'S A volunteer fireman! He must have been there the night of the fire!" Lorrol crowed. "I saw the fire department calendar and his firefighter's certificate back by the bathroom. If we only had a picture of the Fish . . ."

"What *does* he look like, anyway?" I asked.

"Perfect, like we invented him. Eyes far apart, gray hair and speckly skin. And he slides along sideways." Lorrol waved her arms in a swishy way. "Like he's swimming with the current."

"So maybe Mr. Dither would remember seeing someone like that drifting around on the night of the fire."

"Maybe. Should we go back and ask? And I'll describe him?"

"Not now. What if we get Mr. Dither suspicious, and he feels he has to stop us? Grown-ups sometimes get so worried about kids doing their own investigations, you know? Like they don't want us to get hurt." I rolled my eyes as if I did this kind of thing all the time.

"I know," Lorrol said. "He did seem a little nervous. He might freak out about us spying."

We sat on a bench on Elm Street for a few minutes. The sun was high now, and sweat trickled down my neck. I smelled Lorrol's coconut smell, which probably meant she was broiling, too.

"Let's take a break in the library and see if we can figure out any more about the notebook," I suggested. "The Fish has gone to an awful lot of trouble for it."

"And created an awful lot of *tsuris*."

"No kidding. He's gotta know something that we haven't figured out."

"Yet," Lorrol added.

We headed into the always-cool library, which felt like protected territory, probably because of Mrs. Cloozer. Lorrol wasn't holding on to the line, I wasn't being bait, and neither one of us noticed the top of a gray head seated in one of the armchairs not far from the computers.

The Gas Gazette: Issue Fifteen

A FREE NEWSPAPER ABOUT A MYSTERIOUS SOUL

~Starting as a boy, I kept lists and notebooks and crossed things off.

~I stored everything on shelves, in tidy rows and piles.

~I rarely threw out a list.

~I once wrote, "Let the collector's motto be 'Trust nothing to the memory,'" because each moment and experience in life can feel like the best, and the past fades with time. Memory isn't always accurate.

~Lists can tell a story. Here are parts of one of mine from 1859:

> Magnesia. Smelling-salts.

> Little candle. Brandy.

> Thick stockings. Night caps. Shoeing Horn.

> Cigars. Spare Watch & Spectacles.

> Diging shirt. Rough Towels.

> Case to hold Pens and Pencils. Diary.

> Inkstand. Pen-wiper.

> Waterproof coat & Leggings.

> Flask of water. Umbrella. Stick.

~Don't bother to tell me I spelled "digging" wrong.
I'm sure I did.
~Do you feel like you know me better now?

Who am I?

If I saw one of your lists, would I know you better?

NEXT ISSUE TO COME.

FREE!

hunting

LORROL PULLED UP a chair next to mine. I typed *1835 Travel Notebook* into the Search Box.

Up came entries on Mark Twain's notebooks and Nathaniel Hawthorne's, names Lorrol said she'd heard before, and some others we had no idea about. We scrolled to page two. Toward the bottom was:

• *Darwin Online*

"Whoa!" Lorrol and I breathed at the same time. I clicked it.

At the top of the page, under *The Complete Works of Charles Darwin Online*, were choices:

• Publications

• Manuscripts

• Biography

• Credits

"Yikes, this looks hard," I said.

"Yeah, it's for grown-ups, no doubt about that," Lorrol said. "But we can do this. I've read hard stuff before."

"Yeah, plus we're investigating for Darwin *and* us. Think of all the tough things he tackled, not knowing if he'd ever understand them." I had a surge of hope. Gas was just that kind of friend.

"Right." Lorrol nodded. "Click on Manuscripts — that would be handwritten stuff."

I clicked. Up came a long, long list, kind of a chart. Lorrol read the writing on the top: *"This is the largest collection of Darwin's handwritten manuscripts and private papers ever published."*

"The guy sure wrote a lot," Lorrol said.

"He kept a ton of notebooks," I agreed. I thought of my under-the-bed collection, which now seemed very small.

I scrolled on, past the list of drafts and notes for books. Each had a small photocopy of a page next to the entry, and you could click on the word *browse* next to it. It would then get large and you could read more of the real thing, as if you were allowed to step into that notebook.

Whoa, there was a familiar *I*, shaped kind of like a leaf on a long stem, and a bendy *y* that looped up like a fishhook.

"Slow down!" I ordered. "Too fast." Words weren't coming; it was as if my eyes were using all of my brain.

"Like Darwin's tree," Lorrol said, sitting back in her chair. "Branches, and each keeps going. A list tree."

I nodded. Now I spotted a *d* with a squashed top, as if someone had leaned on it, and an *h* with a curly foot. How could this *be*?

Then Lorrol, who read faster than I did, suddenly jabbed the computer screen with her finger. *"Beagle, Beagle!"* she squealed. "We're getting somewhere!"

"Wait!" I said. "Wait! We might miss something!" Actually, I was just waiting for my language to catch up. Lorrol began wriggling next to me. *Squeak, squeak* went her chair.

"Lorrol," I said slowly.

She turned sideways and looked at me.

"I. Know. This. Handwriting."

"You *do*?"

"Maybe everyone old-fashioned wrote that way, but it sure *looks* the same. And I'm pretty good at noticing little stuff, you know I am. I mean, I *memorized* what I saw."

"I believe you." Lorrol nodded.

We scrolled, in silence, through page after page of lists and notebooks.

"Tell me when to stop," she said softly.

I nodded. I don't think either one of us was breathing.

The chart was huge: Gas was clearly a champion record keeper. Suddenly we were looking at a section called "The *Beagle* field notebooks."

"Field Books," I said.

"Ooooh," Lorrol breathed.

There were notebooks that listed names in South America, names I recognized from the little bit of research I'd done so far. Rio de Janeiro . . . Buenos Aires . . . Valparaiso . . .

Then, in one second flat, my whole world came to a stop.

The Gas Gazette: Issue Sixteen

A FREE NEWSPAPER ABOUT A MYSTERIOUS SOUL

~I kept an explosive secret for twenty-two years.

~I didn't think the world was ready to hear it.

~That's a very long time.

Who am I?

NEXT ISSUE TO COME.

FREE!

this is it

"ZOOMY?" LORROL'S VOICE seemed to be coming from outside a bubble, and I was inside.

I reread those three words: *Galapagos, Otaheite, Lima.*

And there, next to the words, was a picture of a cover I knew, complete with torn label. My brain couldn't seem to believe what I was seeing.

I opened and closed my mouth a bunch of times, but nothing came out. Have you ever had an experience so huge that you almost didn't know if you were alive or dead? Well, that was me, lost in

-shock
-hope
-grief

until I flashed on the obvious: I'd found a notebook with a *copy* of the cover of Darwin's Galapagos notebook. The real thing was in some library.

Otherwise they couldn't have scanned it and made this list.

"Dummy" was all I could say.

"Huh?" Lorrol whispered.

"Me." My eyes were still racing along the entry, as fast as they could go, and I then read: *Current whereabouts unknown . . . microfilmed by Cambridge University Library in 1969. The notebook has been missing, presumably stolen around 1983. . . .*

I don't think I will ever have another moment like that in my life.

Explosion is too quiet a word. Suddenly I was soaring, I was floating like an eagle, I was weightless. . . . I was the place where horizontal Deeps meet vertical Deeps and *BOOM!* I was both the FIRE and the CRACK in firecracker.

I was -bigger, -bigger, -bigger than me. Lorrol was patting my arm, but it didn't feel like my arm anymore, it was light and tingly. I knew I wanted to click on the image but my hand wasn't going anywhere.

Lorrol, somehow, knew what to do. I saw her reach for the keyboard.

And there was the first page, with that word, *Benchuca*, circled. I recognized everything. She clicked again: There, miraculously, was the second page. And the third.

Finally, I found some words: "This is it! I had it, I had it, I had it! I HAD DARWIN'S MISSING NOTEBOOK!"

The Gas Gazette: Issue Seventeen

~My secret had to do with how we all came to be who we are.

~I couldn't prove my theory except by collecting more and more data, and that I could do anywhere. I started with the specimens from my trip, and kept going. I wrote to people in faraway places, and asked many questions. Examples popped up wherever I looked, even in my backyard. The more I observed, the more I believed I was onto a Big Idea.

~My wife had a clear vision that she had grown up with. This thought comforted her whenever death took away someone she loved.

~My way of seeing didn't fit with hers. That upset us both.

~I didn't, didn't, didn't want to hurt others with my secret.

~At the same time, I believed it was only a matter of time before it would escape, and I thought it should be shared in the right way.

~After I'd been thinking about this exciting problem

for many years, I told one of my friends that explaining what I saw as life's great puzzle felt like "confessing a murder," as it was likely to horrify and upset so many people.

~It was agony living with such a secret.

~Sometimes logical truth doesn't make the hardest experiences in life any easier.

Who am I?

NEXT ISSUE TO COME.

FREE!

turtles with wings

BEFORE WE CALMED down, Mrs. Cloozer came over and asked if we'd like to play outside. Who knows what we'd been doing — probably hooting and hollering.

And we certainly hadn't seen the man in the armchair stand and walk quietly toward the door.

I was both super-excited and super-sad. And Lorrol believed me. I don't know why or how, but she did.

"You know what feels really shocking?" I asked.

"What?" she said.

"Knowing that Charles Darwin carried that notebook around with him and actually touched every page. Then *I* touched every page, almost one hundred and seventy-five years later. And we were both trying to understand what we were seeing. That's crazy."

"It is." Lorrol nodded.

I told her what my grandpa always says when he's surprised in a good way: *Well, if turtles have wings.*

"Awesome." Lorrol beamed.

I nodded.

Waves of happiness were followed by waves of pain —
I couldn't believe I not only had lost Darwin's notebook,
but had no proof aside from my notes. And who would
listen to a twelve-year-old kid who couldn't see too well?

Lorrol picked up my thinking; not only did we belong
to the Unknown Parent Club and Same Word Club, but we
also seemed to belong to the Reading Minds Club now.

"I know, this hurts. Who's gonna pay attention to a
couple of kids, right? But here's what I think we should
do: Send lots of issues of the *Gas Gazette* to the Darwin
people in England, so they know we're serious researchers, plus just tell what happened. Spill the Beans. So what
if they don't believe us."

"Yeah, the Beans . . ."

"Lots of people say that what Darwin saw on the
Galápagos Islands started him thinking in a different
way, and led him toward his biggest ideas."

"Really?" I asked. I hadn't gotten that far in my
research.

"Yeah, really. The Galápagos are mostly known
because of Darwin's visit. And our friend Gas has gotta
be one of the most famous people in the world."

"And that makes this one of the Most Important
Missing Notebooks anywhere," I said. It felt weird to

have something feel both so good and so bad at the same time. "Think there's a reward?"

Lorrol was quiet for a moment. She shrugged.

I must've looked like a squashed insect, because Lorrol added, "Hey! It *was* in your hands, and I don't think keeping something is nearly as important as finding it. You and I know the truth, and maybe that's what matters in the end."

"Maybe," I said. I looked at my hands. Then I pulled my list book out of my pocket and wrote, in purple pen,

-TURTLES HAVE WINGS.

That helped. Lorrol nodded. "Think I'm going to start doing that," she said. "Keeping lists. Telling myself what's what."

"I'll bring you a couple of my notebooks and pens from home," I said. "We have a supply."

"Thanks," Lorrol said.

"Purple is the color of believing," I added.

When I looked down again, my careful letters had smeared, as if the words were airborne.

planting spuds

THE NEWS SENT *Player Four flying out of town.*

He called the police station, explained that he needed to get home for work reasons, and left his contact numbers. When the Ford truck was released, he'd be back to pick it up. He paid Mrs. Gander's bill and accepted a fresh carrot muffin for the road. Through it all, he felt no joy.

He'd wished on that star, way back in Flint, and now gotten what he wanted. His wish had come true, and it felt rotten.

As he sped past field after field of corn, his window rolled down and the wash of summer sounds and smells pouring in, he felt sad. Very sad. Blue, yellow, green, white, blue, yellow, green, white: the simple colors of a simpler life. Tears prickled in his eyes and he could hear his grandma saying, "Don't forget to plant the spuds! You'll never be sorry." He hadn't understood then, this talk about potatoes, but he did now. Doing a simple, basic thing at the right time mattered.

What had he gotten himself into? Why was he doing what he did for a living?

He'd always been paid well, but was living this way worth it in the end? The player thought of the words on the wall of that elegant office in Dearborn: Survival of the fittest is a deadly game. Who can win forever?

Suddenly he pictured the two kids, unlikely friends in a tiny town, head to head in front of the computer screen. Their wildest dreams had become a reality, but no one would ever believe them. It wasn't even clear, after the fire, that the boy's family would survive.

He hadn't meant to burn down the store after breaking in; he'd heard a noise, dropped his cigarette, and hurried out empty-handed, realizing that the family must have kept whatever was valuable. He'd then watched their home that night, seen the boy hide something in the toolshed, and found the notebook after everyone rushed off to the fire. A quick look around the empty, unlocked house revealed nothing of the right size that seemed more valuable than the odd little book. Poor kid.

The player realized that if he gave back the notebook, that would certainly help, but what was he thinking? Stop. Just play the game, *he told himself roughly. He hoped the package had arrived safely in Detroit. He would never have sent it by regular mail if he'd had any idea what he was sending. . . .*

What luck he'd had! The kids had practically handed him a

huge reward, there had *to be one, if not a juicy price for reselling the notebook on the sly. So why wasn't he happy? Survival was not a pretty business, had he forgotten?*

He frowned, wiped his eyes with the palm of one hand, and stepped on the gas.

melted glass
and blue fingers

MY GRANDPARENTS DIDN'T have any flying turtles to help them through the next few days. Home was quiet, *too* quiet.

"Police found the guy who owns the truck," Gumps announced one morning. "Name's Wade Finner. He was staying with Mrs. Gander, and sure sounds like the creep who came into the store that day."

"Huh!" I said, and tried to look surprised. I couldn't wait to tell Lorrol his real name; *wade* plus *fins* was too perfect.

"They don't have any evidence on him, but apparently the box was some sort of delivery. Anyway, Finner left town, but he'll be back to get his truck when they release it. That was one bad-luck delivery for Buckeye and for us, I'll say that."

"Maybe not so unlucky," I said. Gumps only grunted.

I'd tried to make things better by sharing the amazing notebook news right away, but Gam and Gumps only pretended to believe me. I could tell, and I didn't blame them. After all, what on earth would a lost Charles Darwin notebook be doing in Three Oaks? And wrapped up in a blanket, inside a ratty box, in a truck Buckeye had stolen?

But they were happy I had Lorrol, my first *real* friend, and that she and I were busy at the library every day. I also told them about us making copies of the *Gas Gazette*.

Buckeye was recovering from his burns and also getting help with a serious drinking problem, as the grown-ups called it. There was a lot of his life he plain didn't remember, and my grandpa explained to me that that sometimes happens with alcoholics. Hearing about it, I swore to myself I would never be like that.

We were outside watering the garden, which is a good time to talk about uncomfortable stuff.

"Liquor can make you feel good for a while, then angry, then you mess up and don't even know what you've said or done." Gumps sighed. I thought of Buckeye's threats in the library. Even if he hadn't meant them, how could you trust someone who had been so mean?

"So what'll happen to him?" I asked.

"We won't know for a while," Gumps said. "Buckeye did a mess of destructive things, but sometimes the law allows people to pay in other ways."

"Oh," I said. This didn't sound good. "Do they know yet how the fire started?"

My grandpa then sounded so sad I wished I hadn't asked. "No, and they may never. I guess it burned so hot and everything was so dry that there's not much they can figure out. The police sorted through the ashes."

"Yeah," I said quietly. After a moment I asked, "Is Buckeye ever coming home to live with us?" My voice kind of squeaked at the end of the question.

"Don't you worry about that." Gumps's voice was gruff. "Things will work out as they should."

I tried not to think about it. I couldn't even imagine a less scary version of my maybe-father.

Meanwhile, my grandpa planted like mad and went downtown after lunch every day in his heaviest work boots, armed with rakes and shovels. He was combing the rubble for treasures, and he brought some home.

They were sad to see, but also special. My grandma lined them up on the entryway windowsill: a zucchini-shaped lump of melted blue glass, a plate with an old pair of spectacles stuck to it, and the giant Clydesdale horseshoe, now decorated with chips and flakes of other things. Leftover lives. The last of many family stories.

Gumps was not one for giving up, and he said he wasn't going to rest until everything was fresh as a daisy. He was making that piece of land, land we still owned, real clean. People who had backhoes and dump trucks came to help, and loads of charred wood and twisted metal were hauled away.

"What's the plan?" I asked. I wasn't allowed to go along because there was too much dangerous, sharp stuff underfoot.

"I'm not sure," my grandpa said. "But this is our town and our land and we might just do something with it. Something to help us and other folks."

In that time right after the fire, neighbors were always stopping by our back door, bringing cooked chickens and casseroles. The store burned down on the third of July, and no one in town had the heart to set off any fireworks that weekend. It was the quietest holiday Three Oaks had ever seen. The No Insurance news must've got around real quick, because even though we'd always been a private kind of family, we suddenly weren't alone. Things were changing and that part of it felt good.

The three of us worked extra hard, which left less room for worry crumbs and *tsuris*. I kept my lists detailed and neat and long, hung the wet laundry, made all the beds, then met Lorrol at the library. My grandma went into a baking frenzy and sold a bunch of pies every day. The button jar had to be emptied, and her fingers turned a pale blue from handling so many blueberries; I told her she was evolving into an exotic beetle, and she swatted me with the dish towel.

One secret I held on to was the hunt for Fish. Lorrol and I decided it would only frighten everyone if we told about that day of on-site investigations, but we continued to work full speed ahead in the library.

We both had an odd feeling that if we kept on learning about Charles Darwin, finding and sharing, something big would happen — kinda like a garden giving back vegetables after you've watered the seeds.

the wednesday surprise

ONE DAY AFTER lunch Gumps cleared all of our plates, started to do the dishes, then said, "Naw, this can wait! Who's coming with me?"

Gam and I could tell this was Something. We got ready and hurried out the back door.

As the three of us walked along the sidewalk, I thought about the last time we'd gone this way together — or sort of together, because my grandpa had disappeared ahead. Today the Deeps were beautiful: robin's egg blue overhead, thick green all around, and a just-right breeze that made you feel like nothing terrible could ever happen again.

We'd crossed the train tracks and were close to the empty lot when Gumps said, "Well, I'll be."

At the same time, Gam said, "Oh!" and sounded happy.

"What, what?" I couldn't see any details in the gap where the store had been, but I saw movement.

Here's what was happening: My grandpa had put up a sign. It said,

The Chamberlains thank you for all your kindness.
Feel free to use this Land to barter any goods.
No money will be allowed.
Every Wednesday afternoon is Chamberlain
Whatnots Exchange Day.

Gam clapped her hands after reading it aloud. "You are amazing, Ash Baker Chamberlain!" she said.

We strolled around. People were exchanging things they grew and things they owned, trading by bartering.

Gumps took me over to a corner where he'd set up a plank desk with a crate for a seat. "Thought you might like to keep a record of some of what's bartered, Zoomy. Bought you a fresh record book for the job."

There was a brand-new ledger and two purple pens. "Love to!" I said. "Can I get Lorrol to help? She's terrific at lists, too."

"Of course," my grandpa boomed, looking almost happy. "More the merrier." He went looking for another crate while I found Lorrol at the library.

Here's some of what she and I recorded that afternoon:

- -a bag of winter boots = a bushel of fresh green beans
- -an ice cream maker = a zucchini casserole and a spaghetti pie, both ready for freezing
- -a huge stack of *National Geographic* magazines = a winter parka with fur around the hood
- -a pogo stick = a baby seat for a car
- -a set of bedsheets with a *like new* tag = four steak knives
- -two metal snow shovels = six glazed flowerpots

My grandparents seemed more cheerful than they'd been since the fire, and everyone was chatting.

Out of that terrible hole, that painful place -in our family and -in the row of old buildings on Elm Street, it seemed like something good was growing.

One of the kids at the barter was running around with a copy of the *Gas Gazette*, asking if anyone knew who the Mysterious Soul was. Then Lorrol and I overheard Mrs. Gander saying, "I guess there are issues of this paper coming out all the time. You can find them tucked into books in the library and into the *South County Gazette*. I've read three and I'm looking for more. I wonder if it's a real person being described."

Someone else replied, "No, I don't think so."

"What if it is, and there's a prize if you guess right?" a little kid chirped. "How do you know if you've figured it out?"

Lorrol and I looked at each other.

"A *prize?*" she whispered.

"Now we're in trouble," I whispered back.

The Gas Gazette: Issue Eighteen

~After decades of careful recording, I got a letter from another naturalist, a friend. He had stumbled on the same dangerous solution to this giant puzzle, the one I'd been collecting data on for many, many years. I didn't know what to do.

~I wrote like mad, and finally published my ideas in a book.

~Even though the book became famous, I stayed in my study, at home.

~On the few times I went out in public, I got so nervous my stomach went wild — yup, you guessed it — and I had to rush for the bathroom.

~I believed what I wrote with all my heart, and knew it was important to communicate my insights. But all the arguing started by my ideas made me anxious and upset.

~I didn't like ruining other people's solutions to this same puzzle, even if I disagreed.

~I was always testing pieces to see if they fit with my design. Some did and some didn't. If I was wrong, I was just as interested as if I was right. Sometimes more.

Who am I?

Have you ever been glad to be wrong?

NEXT ISSUE TO COME.

FREE!

a can of guesses

"I HAVE IT," Lorrol announced the next day.

In squeezing past my chair at the library, she knocked my baseball cap sideways on my head. I straightened it out.

"Me, too," I said, "or part of it," and I pulled a coffee can out from under my desk. It had a canning label on it with the words GAS GAZETTE GUESSES, and a slit in the top. "People can write down what they think, with their name and a date."

Lorrol clapped her hands and did a little jump, this time landing on the toe of my sneaker. "Perfect! And here's what I thought of for the prize: Whoever wins gets to write a guest issue of the *Gas Gazette*, put their name on it, and it'll go in our package to England, to the Darwin family! How's that? Fame!"

"Awesome," I said, wiggling my toes to be sure they still worked. "And how about this: Whoever adds to the *Gazette* can then help us decide where to leave the printed copies, and maybe some will be mailed to friends and Gas's stories and ideas will spread across the U.S. and maybe the *world*!"

"Awesome, Zoomy! Brain Boy, that's you!" Lorrol did another jump and must've thrown her arms up in the air, because this time my cap whizzed off.

"Oh, sorry! I'm really beating up on you this afternoon." She giggled as she reached under the table. "Hey, what's this under your chair?"

"I brought the Danger Box. I thought it was just right for storing our work. I cleaned it out and my grandma put some wax paper on the inside."

I handed it to Lorrol. It still smelled like firecrackers. Lorrol took an appreciative sniff. "Awesome." She nodded. Then she pulled a bunch of copies of the *Gas Gazette* from her backpack and put them inside.

We settled in to work, and added more to the pile. At the end of the afternoon, we asked Mrs. Cloozer if we could set up the Guesses Coffee Can on her counter and store the Danger Box down below. She agreed, and offered to lock both in the library's old bank vault every night. She knew the Chamberlain family had had enough losses for a while.

Being a big mystery fan, Mrs. Cloozer helped in other ways. She let us use the library's printer and paper supply, and didn't share our research with anyone — although several bobby pins popped clear out of her hairdo when she realized our project was both factual and filled with secrets.

"You two are *onto* something!" she whispered several times.

We bounced out the door that day. The *Gas Gazette* was coming alive in its own way. I could see now that evolution was part chance, part environment, part odds, part surprise.

I was also starting to see that surprise wasn't all bad. If the notebook hadn't disappeared from the Danger Box, the *Gas Gazette* wouldn't be evolving in this way. If the store hadn't been in trouble, I might not have tried so hard to figure out if the mysterious notebook was valuable.

And if the store hadn't burned down, well . . . that was way too sad to think about, but we definitely had a bumper crop of friends we'd never had before.

The mixture of Bests and Worsts in any kind of evolution sure was confusing.

the good-bad tangle

IF I'D MADE a list of all the good and bad things that happened that summer, I could've used all the purple ink in the Midwestern United States. As it was, I'm sure I used most of it. And I noticed something mighty odd: Sometimes good blurred into bad, and vice versa. The lists got tangled in my mind.

Take Buckeye, for example. The first two times he turned up were horrible, and his trouble with the law was frightening. But I'd started to feel truly sorry and a bit responsible for him. And I could tell my grandparents felt bad in the same way, like maybe they could've prevented some of the things that went wrong in his life.

And then once Lorrol and I spied on the Fish, he escaped, and it looked like he might get away free *and* claim the notebook, I wanted to make things fairer for Buckeye. The way things were unfolding, Buckeye might go to jail and the Fish might be a lucky and famous man. It just wasn't right. So that made me work even harder on telling the Darwin folks the truth.

And here was something positive that turned out to be negative: Finding the old notebook in that beat-up box, and asking to hold on to it for a day or two. That felt like a lucky thing when it happened, and started Lorrol and me on our Darwin research. But if the notebook had been in the blanket, in the box, the way Buckeye left it with us, the store might still be standing. That is, if I hadn't loved notebooks and asked to see it.

So did that make finding the notebook good or bad? Bad, of course, but also good. What if the Fish had never found his opened box in the store? Would he then have watched our house, and found the notebook in the toolshed? Would the store still have burned that night? What if I'd never looked closely at Darwin's notebook, and Lorrol and I had never figured out who wrote it? I couldn't separate the goods from the bads because it seemed like both were in there and they kept changing places. But one thing stayed clear: I wanted that notebook to survive. The store could never be saved, but the notebook . . . well, it was still possible.

It seemed like seeing wasn't a big part of this, because so many things looked like one thing and then turned out to be another. A discovery wasn't always a happy thing and a happy thing wasn't always a discovery. I started to realize that I could figure out plenty without seeing a whole lot.

I was thinking like a palindrome; stuff that went in one direction also seemed to go in the other.

Then Lorrol brought news I didn't expect.

something sneaky

"ZOOMY?"

"What?"

"There's something I've got to tell you." Lorrol wriggled around on the bench outside the library. I didn't like the direction this was going.

"You're leaving and going back to the city." That was about the worst thing I could imagine.

"No, but I did something sneaky. Something I didn't tell you about. I didn't know until now if it would work, and didn't want to get your hopes up."

"WHAT?" I asked, suddenly feeling like an anthill under a shoe. I was starting to go in all directions.

"You know the day we visited the post office and Mr. Dither said he'd already sent everything out?"

"Yes." I was dying to do some chin tapping, but instead pulled out my Daily List Book and wrote -Lorrol Tells.

She waited a moment, then went on, "I asked my mom to stop outside the post office after she picked me up at the library that day. I ran back in and explained to Mr. Dither that I wanted to surprise your family, and could he please get back any of the packages he'd mailed yesterday. He said he'd already called the sorting station to ask, realizing this might be doable."

"Really?" I asked.

"Yes. Then, when I went in the next day, he showed me a small package that looked like the right size. It said, 'Wade Finner,' and gave a street address in Detroit. He explained that he had to get in touch with the sender and tell him the story."

"Whoa," I breathed. "So why did you hide this from me?"

"Because I wasn't sure it would add up! Listen. I know it doesn't look good, but I wanted to give you the best gift ever. Like, just hand the notebook over. Magic, poof! It's back. Then, when I realized I'd started something that might cause even more family *tsuris*, I thought I'd better shut up about it until I consulted with my mom."

"So what did your mom say?" I was feeling better already. Lorrol hadn't done anything I wouldn't do; she'd just started something helpful that was sprouting dangerous leaves. That sure sounded familiar.

"I went out to the car and talked with her. I told her about us suspecting the Fish. She went back in with me and also asked Mr. Dither, who was now all twitchy about the package. Then she tried to explain the truth, hoping that might help: We thought the package was a special notebook, one that had great value to the Chamberlain family.

"Mr. Dither's fingers went wild drumming on the counter. He pointed to a slip of paper, a confirmation label with the sender's phone number on it.

"'I called and left a message,' he said. 'I'll let you know when he calls back.'"

Lorrol told me she groaned, and warned Mr. Dither that this man could be a criminal.

"Poor Mr. Dither looked all confused and worried," she went on. "He said, 'But I can't just give it to you. It's not yours.' And I said, 'It's not his, either!'

"Then Mr. Dither said, 'Why not, if he bought it?'

"'Because I don't think he bought it, he stole it!' That's when Mr. Dither's fingers practically joined the Olympics, they were going so fast."

Here Lorrol paused and took a breath.

"Whoa," I said. "Poor Mr. Dither." I imagined him

handing the package to my grandparents, and them handing it to me. I suddenly felt an inch or two taller. "Lorrol, you're the best friend ever!" I blurted.

"Wait," Lorrol said. "Mr. Dither called the police. After Mom and I left."

"The police!" I said, my heart sinking.

Lorrol nodded. "They took the package and have been holding it. They just talked to my mom — we honestly didn't know until now that they had it. Meanwhile, Mr. Dither says the sender, Wade Finner, phoned back and sounded *really* angry on the phone and muttered something about making sure Mr. Dither got fired. My mom tried to reassure him, but I feel awful that I stirred up this new trouble. And my mom is worried. She wants us to be extra-careful."

"And did you tell Mr. Dither or the police that we think this is one of Darwin's notebooks?"

"No, my mom and I didn't know if that was a good idea. We just told them that it was important and fragile. Now they want to talk with all of us."

It seemed like more and more pieces were falling into place, but I still felt a lump of sadness and now a teeny bit of anger. Not against Lorrol, just against the rules that said this notebook wasn't mine. Even though I'd rescued it. And Lorrol had just rescued it again! And that dream about saving our family; it seemed like we'd been so close to having it come true. Some amazing glory would've been mine. I'd almost let go of all that after the notebook disappeared, but now . . .

It felt kinda like I'd been handed a delicious cheeseburger only to have it snatched away just as I opened my mouth -wide, -WIDE, -WIDE for the first bite. This is a secret, but knowing the notebook was still in Three Oaks made me want to snatch it back. It made me hungry all over again.

"Maybe I'm not so different from the Fish," I said slowly.

"Huh?" Lorrol asked.

"Greedy. Knowing the notebook is nearby makes me want to have it. It was my discovery."

"Yeah." Lorrol sighed. "It's frustrating. But remember: We're investigative reporters. You and me and Gas — he was one, too. And our kind of reporting means a lot of questions. You don't always get the answers. Or get to keep them."

I nodded. She was right. "Lorrol, you're an amazing Firecracker," I said, then we both got embarrassed and she shoved me in the shoulder and I shoved her back. In the next five minutes we sat quietly on that bench, just thinking.

Sometimes side by side feels better than words.

The Gas Gazette: Issue Nineteen

~I wrote a bunch of other books in my lifetime, all looking at pieces of the Giant Puzzle that was once my secret.

~In order to do that, I set up thousands of experiments.

~I collected and dissected barnacles.

~I bred pigeons.

~I became fascinated by orchids and also by carnivorous plants, ones that ate insects or a tiny bit of meat.

~I grew prickly, climbing, and flowering plants, and moved them around the house in biscuit tins and pots. I talked to them.

~I watched my children develop and I studied the behavior of animals at the zoo, especially orang-utans. Their emotions look similar to ours.

~I once placed a container of worms on the piano and observed them when my wife played a note. The worms hated the vibrations, but if the family played instruments and shouted nearby, they didn't seem to mind.

~I never got tired of testing. I was overheard saying, "I shan't be easy till I've tried it." That's me: Once I had a question in my mind I absolutely had to see if there was an answer.

~Some questions stayed questions.

~Tough questions have a beauty of their own, don't you think?

Who am I?

NEXT ISSUE TO COME.

FREE!

a gift

WE FOUND OURSELVES at the Three Oaks police station later that afternoon. There were six of us who'd been asked to come: Gam, Gumps, me, Lorrol, her mom, and Mr. Dither. Officer Nab, who had visited our house both before and after the fire, welcomed us into the back room. Our local policeman, Officer Bagg, manned the phone by the front door. He didn't mind; this was more excitement than usual.

"I want to begin by thanking you for coming so quickly," Officer Nab said formally. We all nodded, wondering what was next.

"This," he said. I couldn't see what he was holding, but heard him move. "Can anyone tell me what this is?"

Gumps cleared his throat, and a bunch of chairs squeaked. Lorrol swallowed, a loud *ga-glump* sound. That made me swallow, too.

"Well, Zoomy and Lorrol have an idea," my grandpa started. "But I'm not sure any of us know for sure."

"Did you open it?" I asked. "If it's our notebook, it's

easy to prove who wrote it. You can see every page online."

"Well," the officer said slowly. "We won't do that while we're all sitting here, but this being an investigation . . ."

No one said a word while paper rustled at one end of the table.

"Careful," I breathed. "It's very old."

The next thing I heard was a couple of *Huh*s, then "Yup, that's the one," from Gam.

Lorrol, who was sitting next to me, clapped her hands and did one bounce. *Scree* went her chair. "Zoomy's the best identifier — give it to him!" she ordered, and bounced again.

Mrs. Shein murmured, "Lorrol, honey . . ." but then a big hand put something down in front of me. Something familiar.

"Ohhh . . ." I said. Picking it up, I took off my glasses and held the notebook in front of my nose.

I read those three beautiful words and smelled the sweet mix of musty paper and history. Lightly and quickly, I touched the cover to my chin, a good-bye tap that I knew Gas would understand. And I suddenly realized, right then and there, that you can't always see what's in front of you no matter *how* you see. At least, not while it's happening. That struck me like ~a bolt of lightning, ~a clap of thunder, ~a tidal wave.

What a thought! It lifted *tsuris*, and somehow freed me. It made lots of what I'd lost feel not lost. Of course, that was true for Gas, too. Sometimes experience gets sifted through time, notebooks, lists, imagination — until it becomes an ingredient in something bigger, or a necessary piece in a puzzle. Until it starts to make sense. Until it's no longer just itself. Had Gas himself put the idea into my head? Maybe he had.

As soon as I realized that how you see and what you hold in front of you doesn't always equal what you understand, not right then, I also knew, in a flash of *ping*ness, that what you experience is yours forever. Yours to keep. Yours to turn over and over in your mind. It's YOURS. As I held the notebook that Charles Darwin had also held, I knew he was giving me something I'd never lose,

~never,

~never,

~never.

I whispered, "Thank you."

I was talking to Gas, but Officer Nab said gruffly, "That's okay, son."

After I handed the notebook back, the policeman slipped it carefully into a clean box along with all the original packaging. "Now tell us what happened," he said, dusting off his hands.

So Lorrol and I did. The story tumbled out, complete with all the details about the notebook having been stolen from Darwin's home in England more than twenty-five years before, and us not knowing it was Charles Darwin's until after it had been stolen again — for at least the third time.

My grandparents and Lorrol's mom apologized to me and Lorrol for not completely believing us; the discovery had just seemed too big. Mr. Dither kept repeating, "Oh, my!"

Then Gumps apologized to the police for not reporting the goods in the garage right away. "Now you've almost caught this — what do we call him — hardened criminal, maybe he'll fess up to starting the fire in our store. And tell how he got his mitts on such a valuable notebook in the first place. Buckeye's no angel, I know he helped himself to a truck, but I don't want to see him punished for another man's crimes. Especially when he ended up saving that notebook by delivering it to us!"

"That would be beyond eggshell in the cake," Gam agreed, and if no one but Gumps and me understood, they were too polite to say.

Mr. Dither, who had been drumming gently on the table, said, "Glad the kids came in and I called you. Who knows, otherwise . . . notebook might've been gone forever."

"It's all quite astounding, how this handful of little moments added up," Lorrol's mom added. "I mean, what if Zoomy and Lorrol hadn't met, and therefore never gone to the post office that day? The notebook wouldn't be here on this table. Not in a million years."

"Well," Officer Nab said, "yes, whatever, certainly, and yes, you can bet we'll use the existence and identity of this notebook to catch Mr. Finner. And I want to say that you each made some — well — unusual decisions here, in this — ah, recovery of the item, but that you each did good." He beamed and nodded. "You did good."

"And you'll return the notebook to the Darwin folks in England?" Mrs. Shein asked.

"Zoomy should write the letter that goes with it!" Lorrol blurted before the officer could reply.

Officer Nab's throat made a deep *rumpa-rum* sound, and he said, "Get that letter over to me tomorrow, son," as if it had been his idea.

I could only nod. I was so relieved and suddenly so happy.

"Oh, Zoomy!" Lorrol grinned.

"Well, if turtles have wings," Gumps said.

As we all stood up to go, I heard Gam add, "Hodilly-hum."

zoomy's letter

Dear Darwin family:

My name is Zoomy Chamberlain and I'm twelve years old.
I live in the town of Three Oaks, population a few hundred
souls, in the state of Michigan in the United States of America.
My town has rescued something that belongs to you and that
you probably thought you'd never see again.

It got rescued by a whole bunch of lucky accidents or
maybe I should say crimes. My father, his name is Buckeye
Chamberlain, has been gone all my life. He struggles with a
serious alcohol problem. Anyway, he's done a bunch of stuff
he barely remembers, and that's why he didn't even know he
had a kid – meaning me – until recently. Anyway, not long ago
he stole a truck outside a bar. Inside that truck was an old
box. Inside that box was your notebook.

My family had a store on our main street, and it was in
Three Oaks as long as anyone can remember. It was called
Chamberlain Antiques and Whatnots. It burned down because

of a terrible fire just two weeks ago. But really, I think it burned down because of your notebook.

You see, Buckeye showed up at home one night, and had some pie and left that mysterious box in our garage. He was drunk, and disappeared again. After a few days, my grandpa opened the box. Inside was the notebook, wrapped carefully in a worn blanket. I asked if I could look at it, because I love notebooks and write in my own every day with a purple pen. (Never mind, that's another story.) My grandparents said yes, and meanwhile my grandpa took the old box and blanket to our store.

I tried reading the notebook later that day and figured out some words. I worked really hard, but it was difficult because of the penmanship. Soon I realized I might have a valuable thing because whoever had kept it had seen the *Beagle*, Darwin's ship, and also been to some of the same places, like the Galápagos Islands.

Then I made my first best friend, Lorrol Shein, she's eleven and a half years old, and she and I did lots of research at our town library. We both really like Mr. Charles Darwin; he's inspiring for kids like us. He did so much, even with a truckload of worry crumbs. Lorrol knows about investigative reporting, and came up with a great idea: We could start a free, mysterious newspaper with facts about Mr. Darwin's life, and leave it around town. We did, and thought it was smart not to say his name or the *e* word – we'd just let people guess. It's called the *Gas Gazette*. I don't need to tell you why.

Now for the bad stuff, or some of it. A man with a sticky voice turned up in our town, and we still don't understand the full story, but he was sniffing around in our store. He recognized the box, opened it, and shook out the blanket. He was angry when my grandpa wouldn't sell it to him. Then he left. My grandpa knew he was up to no good, and told me we had to give the box, blanket, and notebook to the police. I asked if I could keep the notebook for one more night, at home, and give it one last read. He said sure.

That night, our store burned down and it broke our hearts.

The whole town ran outside, and Buckeye was found by the back door of the store, hurt. He said he was trying to stop the fire. He's still in the hospital. When we got home that night, I remembered that I'd left the notebook in a special fruit crate that I have. It's called the Danger Box, and I'd hidden it in our toolshed because that seemed so safe. Our toolshed is behind our house.

Guess what: When I went to get it, I found that someone had stolen the notebook while we were all at the fire. That was the worst night of my life.

Then Lorrol and I searched the Internet and discovered what that notebook really was: one of Darwin's field books. We tried to use me as bait to catch the weird stranger, who was still in town. I'm legally blind but we did okay, except I fell down some stairs and Mrs. Gander had to put nasty stuff on my knee.

Lorrol and I are pretty good detectives, and went to the post office next, to see if the stranger had mailed the package – we realized that he'd be smart to get rid of it. He had.

There's more steps, and everyone helped, but we did get it back. And just now the police called to say they'd arrested the guy with the sticky voice, Mr. Wade Finner. He admitted to breaking into the store and then smoking a cigarette while he was hunting for whatever was missing from the box. He hasn't said he started the fire, but I still think that makes Buckeye look less suspicious. I'm glad.

Since you've been missing this family treasure for so long, we thought we'd better send it right back to you. We're including a couple of issues of the *Gas Gazette* and will send more very soon, okay? Plus a map of Three Oaks and some postcards, in case you want to visit.

There's a sign at the edge of our town that says, "Happy

to Have You, Sorry to See You Go." That's what we're like here, at least most of the time.

And in case you're interested, we had no fire insurance on the store. My grandpa is very upset with himself about that, but he couldn't afford it. So now our garden is much bigger, my grandma bakes and sells a lot of pies and breads, and we have a barter day for the town, right in the empty lot where our store used to be. We'll survive. My grandpa said we might even eat squirrel this winter. I help with everything.

So here you go. We will miss the notebook, but we'll never forget it. Gas is now our very good friend.

Sincerely,

Zoomy (and our whole town)

P.S. I only had one day to do this letter, so I dictated it to my grandma, and she wrote it down. Then she took the letter over to Mrs. Fufty, my teacher, who typed it into a computer and printed it for us. Then I got to sign it with my purple pen and write you this note.

survival

SOME UNEXPECTED THINGS happened after Officer Nab sent that letter and the package. Some things that helped our town survive.

First, reporters started calling us from all over the world. The first time it happened, we got a call from England in the middle of the night. My grandpa shouted into the phone and then hung up. When the reporter called back and Gumps understood what it was about, he kept repeating his "turtles" saying, and the newspaper guy thought Gumps was trying to tell him about a new species in our small town. He kept asking, "What sort of wings?"

Next, journalists from all over the United States started showing up in Three Oaks, and that was good for business. *Very* good. They bought a lot of things, talked with everyone, ate three meals a day, stayed in town, and took a ton of pictures. Mrs. Cloozer was interviewed about the library, Mrs. Gander's whole house was full to the top, Mrs. Fufty told stories about what a good student I was (I'm sure she exaggerated), Mr. Dither was happy because the post office got so much attention, and we had to have extra barter days at the Whatnots Lot in order to sell all of our pies and vegetables. This has been an especially good year for tomatoes, and those heirloom types sell for a bundle. Our button jar is doing okay these days.

Buckeye's the only one who hasn't been interviewed, but I don't think he minds. He'll be able to come home in a few months, after he's done community service for stealing the truck and living in the pharmacy. We're making him a room upstairs, in Gam's old sewing room. We've painted it, bartered for a rug, and added fresh curtains. He says he's a New Man, and will never drink again. I sure hope that's right. I've been to visit him a couple of times in the hospital, and he looks different — some pink burns from the fire, but also short hair and no dirty fingernails. He smiles now, and Gam and Gumps say that makes us look alike. We don't talk too much to each other, we're both kinda shy, but I think we'll make friends. Kin is kin, as my grandparents say, and if he stays healthy he can help a lot with the garden, which is now huge. Gumps says we'll be running a small farm by next summer.

I've realized some interesting things about Buckeye and me and luck.

-First, if Buckeye hadn't stolen that truck and come home with the box, I would never have seen the notebook. Never in a million years. And seeing the notebook was a gift. It certainly changed my life.

-Second, if the fire hadn't happened (and it might not have if the notebook had been in the store instead of home with me), Buckeye would never have ended up in the hospital treatment place. He might have died from alcohol before he got help, so in a way that fire saved his life. And the fire happened because of me holding on to the notebook. It's all connected.

So does that mean we're good for each other? I think it might.

There are still lots of confusing opposites and Deeps in my life but I'm starting to see them in a different way. It's almost like all puzzles have both bads and goods. There's the good of finding Lorrol mixed up with the bad of having her go home at the end of the summer; the good of Buckeye getting better mixed up with the bad of not knowing how it'll be when he's back in our family; the good of getting close to everyone in Three

Oaks mixed up with the bad of losing our store; the good of us all getting a bit famous mixed up with the bad of having to answer the same questions over and over, although I'm kind of teasing about that last one.

When Lorrol goes back to the city in a few weeks, I want to give her my Danger Box. She'll totally love it, I already know, and it'll remind her of all our important times together. We'll keep working long-distance on the *Gas Gazette*. Plus, we're still -waiting, -waiting, -waiting to get a "Special Package" that the Darwin family is mailing back to us. I can't imagine what it is, but I can tell they're excited about me and Lorrol receiving it. They keep phoning to ask if it's arrived yet. Mr. Dither will call us right up when it does.

Gas taught us that lists can take you pretty far in life, and Lorrol and I will keep making all of our lists in purple pen. I've gotten her addicted to it. Now that I know Lorrol, I can't imagine stuff happening without her, like we're members of the same species who need each other to survive. Does that mean we've evolved? I don't know, but don't tell; that's a secret question. Secrets you can control, at least sometimes, and life you can't — at least, not always.

Everyone in Three Oaks thinks Gas would've liked our town and been surprised by all the fuss over his little notebook. He's now a friend to us all, and there's no pebble in the pie that can change that.

The turtles are already flying.

an invitation

WHEN THE PACKAGE finally arrived, Lorrol and I ripped it open. There were gifts of all sizes inside, wrapped with paper and ribbons, and THIS LETTER. Sealed in a fancy envelope with a red blob of something called "sealing wax" on the back, it took us ages to decode, but every minute was worth it. Here it is:

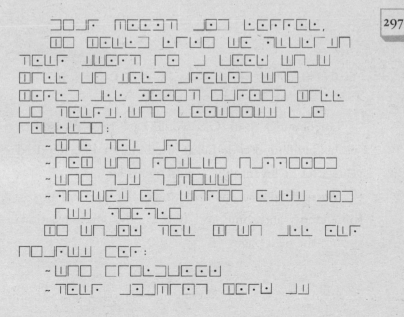

Lorrol and I think Gas would have been pleased to see his childhood code being used almost two hundred years after he invented it — and by his family.

We noticed that the code looks like parts of boxes, some empty and some not. If you want our translation, turn to the next page.

Dear Zoomy and Lorrol,

We would like to publish your story in a book that will be sold around the world. All money earned will be yours. The contents can include:

- who you are
- how the rescue happened
- *The Gas Gazette*
- photos of Three Oaks and its people

We thank you with all our hearts for:

- the Fieldbook
- your amazing work as investigative reporters

We will help by sending a home computer plus Internet for each of you, and microphones so that you can also tell the story by talking.

Please visit us at Mr. Darwin's home in England any time. We will pay all expenses for you and your families.

Sincerely,

The Darwin Family

The Gas Gazette: Issue Twenty

A FREE NEWSPAPER ABOUT A MYSTERIOUS SOUL

~My wife and I loved each other, our many kids, and our home in a little town not far from a big city.

~Our children were brought up to be kind but not quiet.

~They ran, tipped over chairs, jumped on sofas whenever possible, and tried out swearwords. Lots of games happened inside the house. They were allowed to imagine and explore as long as they didn't hurt others.

~Sometimes a guest invited to lunch was shocked at how free the children were.

~Often they came into my study while I was working, and did drawings or curled up on my sofa to rest.

~They liked to be with each other, and with us. They grew by dreaming, questioning, playing, and thinking.

~Some helped me with experiments.

~When I was old, I wrote to my one of my sons that I'd been wondering about "what makes a man a discoverer of undiscovered things." I told him that I thought "the art" was in searching for "the causes and meaning of everything."

~If you live this way, you'll never be bored, I promise.

~There will always be a Danger Box to open.

Who am I?

NEXT ISSUE TO COME.

FREE!

AUTHOR'S NOTE:
what's real

THREE OAKS IS REAL; my characters are not. I've only visited this wonderful and unique Michigan town, but I'm always happy to return and sorry to go. I wrote what felt right and true. My apologies if I've trespassed in any way.

I read a huge amount about Gas's life, and tried to be as accurate as possible. All of the facts about him and the missing item — I'm trying not to give too much away — are one hundred percent real, with the exception of one detail I left out: a small label with the number 63.5 and Gas's name inside the front of the item, an entry perhaps added long after the original was complete. This detail, although remembered by some researchers, isn't visible in the only recorded image and so I didn't include it in the plot of my book. The quotes in the *Gas Gazette* were taken directly from Gas's published and unpublished writings, letters, and notebooks. The words and phrases Zoomy picks out of his secret "find" are all truly there, and can be found online.

English Heritage, the owner of the missing item, has issued a public plea for the return of this treasure. It is also listed as stolen property in *The Art Loss Register*. I hope, hope, hope that one day this hugely important piece of history will be returned to Gas's study, and to the house outside of London where he and his family lived. When and if that happens, there will certainly be a different story to tell and a new Danger Box to investigate.

THE QUOTES:
where to look

A LIFETIME OF READING about Charles Darwin, his world, and his family is now available free and online, thanks in part to the generosity of The Darwin Archive at Cambridge University Library, English Heritage, and many surviving members and friends of the Darwin family. Anyone with access to a computer can enter "Darwin Online" or "Darwin Correspondence Project" and exit with countless original treasures in mind. Try it!

Here's the part where I give you a bunch of titles and numbers — if you're doing some digging, this is your paragraph. All of the words and phrases quoted in the *Gas Gazette* really *were* written by Gas himself. Most were drawn either from *The Autobiography of Charles Darwin* (first published in 1887), Adrian Desmond and James Moore's *Darwin*, a detailed plum pudding of a portrait (1991), or *Darwin and Henslow: The Growth of an Idea*, edited by Nora Barlow (1958). The Darwin quote on the frontispiece is from a letter written to Joseph Hooker in 1844, in "Darwin Correspondence Project," 729.html; the code on page 38 can be found in Cambridge University Library, at DAR 271.1:10, and appears on a sheet of paper dated 1819–21; the entries in the list on page 240 can be seen in "Darwin Online" at CUL-DAR 210.9.30; the phrases quoted on page 300 are from a letter written in 1871, to one of the Darwin sons. Deborah Heiligman also quotes this letter in her marvelous *Charles and Emma* (2009). Should anyone need it, I have a list of the sources for all Darwin quotes that appear in *The Danger Box*.

Each word and phrase that Zoomy collects from his find can be seen in the real thing, which is in "Darwin Online" at EH1.17. It's an amazing experience to look at page after page.

Getting to know my subject happened while reading countless documents and excellent books, and if I have neglected to credit anyone appropriately, it is entirely due to the "sublime" (as Gas might have said) experience of plunging headlong into another world, and of creating the Danger Box that you now hold. A beetle or two may have gotten away from me, but not to my knowledge.

ACKNOWLEDGMENTS:
who helped

THE LIST IS LONG, and lots of people helped me in many, many ways. Without their generosity and input, this book would not have evolved as it did. Thank you all, with all my heart. I'm sorry if I have forgotten anyone — this book was in the making for a number of years, and passed through many stages. Here are some of the people I owe:

-Joshua Patner, for the spark

-Barbara Engel, great friend times ten

-My husband, Bill, our three kids, and both sides of our big family, for everything

-Anne Troutman, for all we continue to share, both visible and not

-Doe Coover, terrific agent, observant reader, and valued friend

-My esteemed editor and buddy David Levithan, like Gas, a gentle and wise firecracker-maker

-Garry Lange, Liz Lange, and the many gifted teachers I met at the River Valley Schools

-John Gunner Gooch, for enthusiasm, fact-checking, and his inspiring *South County Gazette* articles

-Dr. Louise Sclafani, optometrist and professor at the University of Chicago, for helping me to glimpse Pathological Myopia

-Dr. Alison Winter, neighbor and professor of history at the University of Chicago, for thoughtful solutions at the right time

-Dr. Paul White, of the Darwin Correspondence Project, for

checking the Cambridge University filing numbers on a document that is not online

-Bob Strang, for armloads of books by and about Darwin

-David Magill, director of the University of Chicago Laboratory Schools, and the tireless librarians at Lab, for invaluable access

-Angela Sherrill, one of the wizards at 57th Street Books, for reconnaissance and encouragement

-My amazing friends at Scholastic, in addition to David Levithan — and there are many! — in particular, Ellie Berger, Suzanne Murphy, Charisse Meloto, Marijka Kostiw, Tracy van Straaten, John Mason, Robin Hoffman, Stephanie Nooney, Lisa McClatchy, and, last but not least, Dick Robinson, whose thoughtful twinkle reigns.